# Second Chances

### Jordan Austin

**Outskirts Press, Inc.**
**Denver, Colorado**

This is a work of fiction. The events and characters described herein are imaginary and are not intended to refer to specific places or living persons. The opinions expressed in this manuscript are solely the opinions of the author and do not represent the opinions or thoughts of the publisher.

Second Chances
All Rights Reserved.
Copyright © 2008 Jordan Austin
V2.0

This book may not be reproduced, transmitted, or stored in whole or in part by any means, including graphic, electronic, or mechanical without the express written consent of the publisher except in the case of brief quotations embodied in critical articles and reviews.

Outskirts Press, Inc.
http://www.outskirtspress.com

ISBN: 978-1-4327-2734-5

Outskirts Press and the "OP" logo are trademarks belonging to Outskirts Press, Inc.

PRINTED IN THE UNITED STATES OF AMERICA

Renée looked understandingly at Seth. Now it was all starting to make sense. Helping out at the soup kitchen, coaching soccer, volunteering his time and energy; it was all an attempt to give back, a way to say thank you for what had been given to him- a second chance. He had a new lease on life, and with it, he had the ability to intuitively handle all types of absurd problems and situations at which others might be baffled. She rested her head on his shoulder. She wanted to tell him of the love she had for him, how at first she thought it was a mere crush, a foolish attraction, but over time she knew it was so much more. She had fought the feelings, not believing that anything good would come out of her acting on them. There was so much about him which she loved: his smile, his eyes, his sense of humor, his honesty and integrity. But most of all, she loved that fact that he was her best friend. She turned to him with love in her eyes and a deep felt intensity in her heart, but he had fallen asleep. Instead of trying to wake him, she curled up under his arm, thanking God for all the gifts which He had given her.

For all the women and men who have been in verbally, emotionally, or physically abusive relationships and have had the strength and courage to get out before it was too late.

Dedicated to my husband, Scott,
without whom this book would never have been written.

# Prologue

The sun shone brightly through the window as the curtains danced in the light spring breeze. Resting on top of their large bed, Renée lay on her stomach, ankles crossed in the air behind her. Her hair fell around her face, down to her shoulders, as she intently studied a classic car magazine. She ran her fingers over the pictures, imagining what it would be like to drive them . . . a red 1959 Cadillac Sedan Deville, a white 1966 Chevrolet Nova, a yellow and black 1971 Ply Cod. In her opinion, they were all masterpieces. But her favorite was a metallic blue 1969 Chevy Camaro. "Wow," she whispered to herself. She smiled as she dreamed of someday sitting in the driver's seat.

"Looking at those stupid car magazines again? Why do you waste your time with that? You get ticked off at me for having porn magazines in the house, but they're a hell of a lot more interesting than that," Mel said walking into the bedroom, rudely disturbing Renée's daydream. Mel's sharp, blue eyes were slightly blood shot, and to Renée's dismay, he had recently shaved off his blonde hair for what he considered to be a more becoming look. Unfortunately, it hadn't worked. Instead of looking macho and tough like he had presumably intended, he looked like an oversized cue ball.

"I will have a car like this someday," Renée assured him. "You'll see." She rolled onto her back, crossed her legs, and continued to page through the magazine.

"Sure you will, baby," Mel answered condescendingly. "Sure you will. You just keep dreaming those stupid dreams. I just don't get you, Renée," he said with his back to her, rummaging through the dresser drawer for a t-shirt, "you're never satisfied with what you have. Why can't you just realize that this is about as good as life gets? Why can't you be happy with what you have instead of wanting everything that you don't?"

"That's not true, Mel," she said as she set down the magazine to look at him. "I am grateful for all I have, for all we have. But don't you have dreams? Aren't there things that you'd really like to see happen in your life?" she imploringly questioned, hoping maybe this time he would come to see her point.

"Yeah," he replied matter-of-fact as he sat on the edge of the bed and pulled on his socks. "Yeah, I would like to have a fiancé who isn't so selfish. One who would think more about my needs and not so much about hers. Is that the kind of dream you mean? Is that what you're talking about, Renée?" He turned to face her, but Renée, sitting cross-legged, magazine lying in her lap, hung her head like a child after being reprimanded and did not say anything. Mel stood up and checked his reflection in the full length mirror hanging on the back of the bedroom door. He was on the thinner side, and less than average in height, only about three inches taller than Renée. But what he did not have in stature, he definitely made up for in ego. Searching for his watch on top of the dresser, he continued, "You know you're really selfish. When I need something, you never seem to want to help me out, just look at all I've done for you!"

Renée took a deep breath and questioned, "What is it this time, Mel? What do you need?"

Mel turned to her and shot her his best smile. "I just need a few bucks. I've a few things I need to get."

"But, Mel, you said you got paid yesterday. What happened to the money?" She looked at him with perplexity. It was always about money with him. She had been scrimping and saving, trying to make ends meet, and Mel always needed money.

"Well, last time I asked, you wouldn't give me any, so I had to ask a guy I know from work for a loan. When I got paid, I gave it to him." He had such an uncanny way of making her feel small and weak, like she had done something wrong. "See, Renée, if you wouldn't have been only thinking of yourself, if you wouldn't have been so selfish, I wouldn't be in this position. It's not my fault, it's yours."

Reluctantly uncrossing her legs, lifting herself off the bed, and walking across the room, Renée opened the small, wooden jewelry box on top of her dresser. "Here, this is all I have," Renée said taking out a twenty dollar bill she had put away in case of an emergency and handed it to Mel, "take it." From past experiences, Renée knew it was easier to give in to Mel than to try and stand up for herself. Because of the cruel way in which he had been increasingly treating her, she dared not anger him by saying no.

There were many days she wondered how she could have gotten herself into the situation in which she was. Early in their relationship, he had been so charming, so charismatic. He had paid attention to her needs and wants, and he had truly shown an interest and listened when she had talked. But as with the wave of a hand, things had begun to change. The flowers he used to bring home "just because" were soon replaced with insults and putdowns. His once kind and understanding demeanor had been supplanted with sarcasm and hostility.

"I'm leaving," Mel said snatching the money from Renée's hand. "Don't wait up for me either 'cause I'll probably be out late."

"Where're you going?" Renée asked quietly as she anticipated his response.

"What? Are you my keeper now? I'm just going out. That's all you really need to know," he said over his shoulder as he walked out of the bedroom door.

Renée sat on the edge of the bed, put her head in her hands, and felt the tears roll down her cheeks. (*Why did he have to be so cruel?*) She sat for a few moments, sadly thinking over the question for which she could not come up with an answer, and rubbed her fingertips against her temples in an attempt to relieve the tension that was growing. As she sadly lifted her head, she heard Mel start his car and take off out of the driveway.

That night Renée lay awake. It was late, and Mel was not home. She looked at his side of the bed still neatly made, glanced at the clock, and wondered where he could be. Lately, he had been coming home later and later. When Renée would ask him where he had been, he would cut her off snapping, "If it was your business, I'd tell you."

Renée was tired; so very tired of the ups and downs of their relationship. (*Maybe*, she thought as she lay on her pillow, *maybe it's partly my fault. Maybe I expect too much of him. Maybe I haven't shown enough patience or tolerance.*) Renée could not figure out the hold that Mel had over her. (*No one in her right mind would put up with the way he treats me, so am I insane?*) "No," Renée whispered, desperately trying to convince herself, "I just believe that there's good in everyone." Unfortunately, this belief had gotten her deeply involved with a man whom she was supposed to marry, but one whom she did not always feel she loved. When he was not thinking only of himself, displaying selfish and self-centered behavior, he was everything for which she had hoped in a husband. He could be kind, considerate, understanding, and compassionate. When he was committed to a project that was important to him, he could be a hard worker and diligent about completing the task. However, there had been a change in him. Although Renée earnestly tried to understand, the only conclusion that made any sense was that they had grown apart. At the time of their engagement, she had believed that they wanted the same things from life. But as the days went by after he had gotten down on one knee, placed a diamond on her finger, and had promised her the world; things had not been the same. She wondered if she had she rushed him into a decision into which he wasn't ready to make. She pondered the thought as she stared at the ceiling almost expecting to see an answer in the plastic stars illuminated by the moonlight. No, was her final consensus. When they had started dating, she had not been looking for anything serious. In fact, she had just gotten out of a relationship, and she had been, for the first time in a long time, enjoying the freedom of the single life. He had been the one who had been so determined to begin a life with her, or so it had seemed. Although there had been a definite beginning, starting with getting engaged and then buying a house, Mel's obvious lack of respect and integrity was not what Renée was going to accept. The life for which she was wishing was not one filled with extravagance, but one filled with the hopes and dreams of many people- getting married and having some children. (*But it's difficult*, Renée realized, *to make dreams come true when only one person is working towards the goal.*)

"When is it going to be my turn?" Renée questioned quietly into the darkness. She was watching the shadows from the moonlight shine through the bedroom window. As the tears began to slide down her cheeks, with desperation in her voice, she uncertainly asked, "God? God, can you hear me? Are you really there? If you are, why won't you help me?" She exhaled loudly. "You know everything, so you probably understand that I'm doing the best I can just to hang on right now." She took a breath in an attempt to calm herself. "Hey, God, I'm sorry. I don't mean to sound so bitter, but I just don't get it. I believe that things happen for a reason, and I believe you bring people into our lives for a reason. So if Mel is really supposed to be a part of my life, then why does he often treat me so badly? Am I really doing everything so wrong? Why can't things work out between us? Do you really want me to be alone? Because if you do-no offense, God- I don't think that's really fair. I look around at others, and it's difficult for me to accept that they have what I want."

Renée sat up, brushed her hair away from her face, pulled her knees into her chest, and continued to whisper, "Maybe you're just wondering what I want. Could that be it?" She lightly rocked back and forth as she thought it over. Then she said very softly, "All I'm really asking, God, is to be happy . . ."

She laid her head on her knees and sighed as she began to tenderly speak her thoughts, "What would bring me happiness? Happiness would be coming home from work to a loving husband who would ask me 'How was your day?' Watching the man I love sleeping beside me, instead of wondering where he is all night, and waking up next to him in the morning. Filling our home with the laughter of children who we will love and raise with Your guiding hand. Having enough money to pay our bills instead of wondering if there'll be enough money each month to pay the mortgage and put food on the table. Living each day with the understanding that it is on loan, a gift from You, to use the best we can and encourage others to do the same."

Renée stopped for a moment and desperately pleaded, "God, is this too much to ask? Is it that I'm not deserving of a life like this? Others have it. Why can't I?" She let out another sigh, tilted her head so she could look up at the ceiling, and compliantly added, "I know, I know. I know that I have to be patient, but when is it going to be my turn?" She sat up a little straighter and said with conviction, "And you know, God, when it is my turn, I promise I'll never forget You, and I'll always be grateful for everything You've given me . . ." She waited, almost for an answer, and then regrettably continued, "God, there are times I feel deep in my heart that maybe Mel's not the man who's going to give me these things. If he's not, I pray that You'll grant me the strength and courage to let him go." Renée sighed one last time, lay back on her bed, and fell into a deep sleep.

# Chapter I

It was Saturday, the end of April. The spring day was not just warm . . . it was hot. The grass was turning green, and buds were beginning to appear on the trees. Maggie, a friend of Renée's, needed a place to stay. Maggie had been Renée's hair stylist for many years. During this time, the two of them had gotten to know each other fairly well. Renée had always liked Maggie because of her spunk and her straight-forward, honest personality. So even in view of Mel's objections, Maggie was moving in. But of course, her stay would only be temporary although their home had more than enough room to have a guest. Renée was very proud of her house, particularly due to the fact that she had worked so hard to get it to look like it did. She had thoroughly gone through the house, revamping each room. The task had consumed a great deal of her time and energy, but the end product was well worth the effort it had taken.

When she and Mel had moved in, she knew the house would need work, but she had been uncertain as to how much. But it was theirs, and she had endeavored each night after she had gotten home form work and ultimately transformed the house into a beautiful home. Since they had moved in in February, Renée had decided she had about two months to transpose the interior, and then in the spring, her next conquest would be the fenced in backyard. It had a lot of potential, but this too would take a lot to meet with her satisfaction. Sadly, the previous owners had not taken the greatest care with their property.

Painting walls, pulling up old, shag carpet, sanding and varnishing floors were just some of the pains she had to endure when she had begun the interior desecration. The front porch had been filthy, but when she had scrubbed and painted it, it took on a new aura. She happily had hung crisp, white ironed curtains on the large windows. She had found a bench and had placed it along the wall. It added warmth and practicality to the porch; a place where a person could sit down and take off his boots. Slightly old fashioned, but Renée liked it.

The kitchen was small and led into a dining/living room area. Finding odds and ends and wall fixtures at discount stores had tied everything together giving the main floor a very warm, inviting feeling. Renée was amazed at how much elbow grease and a couple of coats of paint could change the look of an entire room. Renée had been delighted when she had found a bargain on a wooden dining room table with four matching chairs. She had always felt that it was important to have a table at which a family could eat meals together. Unfortunately, she and Mel were not in the habit of doing so, but it was her hope that this would change over time.

The master bedroom was also on the main floor next to the small bathroom. In it large windows had been covered with dusty window shades. Renée had taken them down, sewed curtains, hung them up, and let the sun shine into the room. The bedroom set she had found was not new, but again, Renée was amazed at the power of varnishing and staining.

Renée really liked the layout of their home. Coming in from the porch, there were stairs that led to the downstairs. With help from a friend, a carpenter by trade, the two of them had sketched in an additional bedroom on this level. The remaining rooms were a bathroom, laundry area, and furnace room. There was also a nice sized family room that Renée imagined someday would be filled with the laughter of children. If one went back up the stairs to the main floor and turned towards the living room, behind a wooden door was a staircase that led to the upstairs bedrooms. Large windows welcomed the sun, and the hard wood floors, now refinished, were beautiful.

"Oh, thank you, thank you," Maggie said walking though the door of the small, two-story house. In her arms was a boxful of items. "Should I take these up to *my room*?" She smiled brightly, as she looked at Renée.

"Yes, yes, just up the stairs. You know where it is. . ."

"Oh, this is my friend, Seth. He's going to help me move in."

Seth looked up from under his light blue baseball cap, and Renée's brown eyes met with his. She felt slightly weak in the knees, and as much as she didn't want to admit it, she felt her heart skip a beat. "Nice to meet you," he shyly said with a smile.

Renée embarrassedly turned away and mumbled, "Yeah, you too . . . ah, you can just follow Maggie."

He nodded, and Renée watched him walk up the old, wooden, enclosed staircase to Maggie's room. Shaking her head from side to side and letting out a breath, she held onto the railing to steady her knees as she began to regain her composure. (*What just happened?*)

"New friend of yours?" Surprised, Renée turned to see Mel standing behind her. His arms were crossed over his chest, as he glared at her with disdain on his face.

"Huh?" she asked still trying to gain her composure. "Oh, Seth?" she asked as nonchalantly as possible. "He's just a friend of Maggie's."

"I know who he is, and," he said leaning closer to her, "if I were you, I would stay away from him. You understand?" he questioned menacingly as he grabbed her arm, slightly twisting it.

"Yes," she answered as she winced from the pain. "Please let go, you're hurting me." She looked into his penetrating blue eyes, and again, she felt the same uncertainty arise. (*What am I doing with him? What have I gotten myself into?*)

"Go put some clothes on, you look like a whore," Mel remarked looking at her up and down. He released her arm and walked into the living room to his usual spot, the overstuffed orange chair, where he would reside for the remainder of the day, and into the night, playing video games.

"Dear God," Renée managed to say as she quietly shut the bedroom door behind her, "please help me. I know I got myself into this, but please, God, help me to get out." She looked at her reflection in the mirror. As her eyes stared back at her, they reflected her sadness and uncertainty. Not even a hint of the usual mischievous sparkle was present. Her long, light brown hair was tied back, and she shrugged her shoulders at what she was wearing. Earlier she had been working in the yard. She loved spring. The fresh smells, the sight of all God's creations coming to life in anticipation of the warm, nurturing days ahead of them. Cleaning away the debris that had accumulated in the yard over the winter, she had dressed casually in a pair of old, cut off Levi's and an old white t-shirt that had been Mel's. Hurt and frustrated with his comment, she begrudgingly changed into jean shorts that came just above the knee and grabbed a pink, loose fitting t-shirt. "No sense provoking him when he's in one of his moods," she said quietly as she slipped the shirt over her head. Then she left the room to see if Maggie needed any help with unpacking.

"So is Renée a good friend of yours?" Seth asked casually, carefully walking up the stairs carrying yet another box of Maggie's filled with socks, books, magazines, and what looked to be her leftover lunch. He peered questionably into the box and glanced over at her. His intent was to ask her if this was the way she usually packed, but seeing the frustration on her face of trying to organize her belongings, he decided against it. Besides, he didn't want to distract her. He was intently waiting for her to reply to his (hopefully casual) question about Renée.

The upstairs off the house was fairly open with a bedroom, where Maggie was to stay, adjacent to the larger area that served as a sitting room. The sitting room was Renée's favorite area in the house. There she found solitude when she needed a break from the real world. Wanting it to somewhat resemble a study, she had found an old table that served as a desk, and placed it against the wall by the window. When shopping, she had been delighted to find two old style looking chairs, that although were not the kind one could sink into, they were comfortable when sitting and drinking tea or coffee. Although she was the first to admit that she was anything but a professional artist, on the wall she had hung the pictures she had painted. Painting was a pastime that she had really come to enjoy.

"Uh, yeah," Maggie replied as she flipped one blonde braid over her shoulder. "I guess I've known her for some time. She was in the shop the other day. As I was cutting her hair, I told her about my situation, and that I needed a place to crash for a while. Probably only a couple of weeks, a month, I didn't know." She continued to try and sort through her things, then looked seriously at Seth. "She also confided in me that their financial situation isn't the greatest after Mel quit his job. So me staying here would help her out a lot. Although she was hesitant, I-of course- told her I'd pay her something for rent."

"Oh," Seth replied. "Why'd he quit?"

"She really didn't say much. I got the feeling that she was pretty embarrassed about the whole thing. Either way, it'll benefit us both. But I'm glad it's only for a few weeks. Mel gives me the creeps. He has from the first time I met him. What do you think she sees in him anyway? He's got scary eyes, don't you think?"

"Yeah," Seth replied as he set down a box, "that's not all that's scary about him."

"Huh?"

"Oh, never mind." Seth seemed to be temporarily lost in thought. After a moment, he continued, "It's just that I've known Mel for quite some time. We used to run in somewhat the same circle. Well, I basically ran the circle, and he ran circles trying to keep up with us. But hey, people change, right? Maybe he has, too."

"Whatever," Maggie replied not really paying much attention to what Seth had said. "Change or no change, I think he's a jerk. Personally, I hope she tells him to get lost."

"Sometimes that's a lot easier said than done," Seth said almost under his breath but loud enough for Maggie to hear.

She turned to him and said with a look filled with genuine sympathy, "Oh, that's right. I heard you finally got rid of. . ."

"Kathy," Seth finished the sentence for her.

"Yeah, she was a real piece of work," Maggie said as she began unpacking some more boxes. Not feeling sorry she had spoken the truth, but feeling slightly bad that it came out so harshly, she lightly laughed and added, "I mean, as if you didn't already know that. But hey, we all live and learn, right?"

"Something like that," Seth said as he glanced at the paintings that were hung on the wall. As he walked closer to them, he realized they were ones Renée had painted herself, as her signature was scribbled at the bottom of each one. Giving them a look of approval, he nodded his head and said, "Hum." Turning his attention to Maggie, he deliberately changed the subject by teasing her. "I thought this was a temporary move. Why are you bringing all this stuff?"

"Well, I have to have. . ." However, Seth didn't pay attention to the rest of her sentence. As he was glancing out the window located at the far end of the larger room, he saw Renée playing with her little white and black dog. (*Wow, she sure is beautiful.*) But it wasn't just the outward beauty that had made his heart seem to stop when he had first seen her. Sure she was a very attractive woman with her light brown hair, large brown eyes, and petite, athletic build. But he knew instinctively it was more. Her smile had completely captivated him. Looking into her eyes, it was as if something inside him had awoken; something that he did not even know existed. He shook his head from side to side. (*I have to stop thinking like this. After all, she's engaged. Yeah, engaged to a psychopath, so what does that tell me about her?* Seth wondered if it was just self-pity that made him refer to Mel in that manner.) As stated by Maggie, his ex-girlfriend was quite a piece of work. Even now, she still couldn't take no for an answer and realize that Seth was trying his best to move on with his life. Kathy had been so relentless in calling him over and over that it had resulted in him having to change his number.

". . . Seth? Seth? Earth to Seth? Did you hear anything I said?" Maggie shot him an annoyed look. "Well?"

"Well, what?" He said as he reluctantly turned away from the window. He was pretending that he was trying to cool himself from the slight breeze. Although he and Maggie had been friends for a long time, he was not going to convey to her the irrational feelings he was having.

"Do you have any other plans for the day, or are you going to hang out here and help me unpack?" Maggie, still slightly annoyed at Seth's obvious inability to stay focused, questioned, "Are you going to be spacey all day? If you are, I can move my things myself." She sighed, trying to let go of her frustration and remember that Seth had given up his Saturday afternoon to help her.

"I'm fine," Seth lied. "I'm fine." He annoyingly removed his baseball hat, ran his hand through his dark hair, and placed the hat back on his head. "I guess I just have a lot on my mind."

"Okay, I'm sorry. I just hate being ignored." She gave Seth a quick hug and said, "Thank you for being here. Should we go get the rest of my things?"

As she and Seth left her room and were heading down the stairs, they literally ran into Renée.

"Are you okay?" Seth asked as he held Renée by her shoulders until she regained her footing on the narrow stairway. He looked down at her, as he was about a foot taller, and said, "Sorry, we were just on our way out to get another load."

"Yeah, I'm okay. Sometimes this stairway can be a bit tricky." She looked up at him and teasingly added, "Especially when you're built like a pro football player."

(*There it is again. The same feeling I had gotten the first time I had seen her.*) Seth smiled and embarrassedly mumbled, "If you say so." Then he walked carefully past her down the stairs. He was anxious to get outside into the fresh air.

"He's kind of . . . I don't know . . . kind of out of it," he heard Maggie comment to Renée. "I don't think he's been sleeping so well since . . ." Her voice trailed off and Seth was glad he didn't get to hear her finish her sentence. He had had enough of people feeling sorry for him. Yes, it had been a rough break up, but he and Kathy were done. The relationship had drained him every way possible, and he knew without any uncertainty that he had truly made the right decision by ending it.

"Seth, long time no see," Mel said as he came outside and lit a cigarette. "So what do you think of the place?"

"It's nice, really nice," Seth acknowledged looking around.

"You really think so?" Mel said leaning against the rail of the deck, "I think it's just a glorified apartment. I don't know what I was thinking when I let Renée talk me into buying it, but you know women. They always seem to get their way. Don't you think?"

Seth forced a smile and answered with little emotion, "Sure." (*You ungrateful jerk. This house is much more than a glorified apartment.*) The white two-story house could use some work, but it had character. Bringing in Maggie's things had given him a chance to look around. In doing so, he could tell that someone, probably Renée, had put a lot of work into transforming the house into a home. (*Why is it that some people are never grateful for what they have?*)

"So," Mel said tipping back on a deck chair while crossing his legs on the railing, "how are you and . . . ah," he snapped his fingers as if it would help him remember. "What's her name doing?"

Seth looked down and absent-mindedly kicked some rocks from the driveway and said, "Kathy." Then he reluctantly continued, "Uh, not so good. We aren't together anymore."

"Oh?" Mel flicked his cigarette butt into the yard. "That's too bad, man. Yeah, women can be a real pain in the ass sometimes, can't they?"

Seth shrugged his shoulders. He never had particularly liked Mel, and he really didn't feel like talking about his personal life with him. He looked at Mel and wondered what a women like Renée could see in a guy like him.

"So," Mel butted into Seth's thoughts, "since the two of you aren't together, how about giving me her number?"

"What?" Seth asked in surprise.

"Hey, I was only kidding, man." Mel laughed as if he

had told the funniest joke he had ever heard. "Lighten up. There are plenty of women out there, plenty."

"Yeah, easy for you to say, look who you're going to marry."

"Ugh, don't remind me." Mel abruptly set down the chair on which he was rocking. "Yeah, Renée can put on quite a show of being really sweet, but wait until you get to know her. She can be a real bitch." He continued rocking in his chair, sighed, and with a *feel-sorry-for-me* look added, "But hey, I guess a guy has to settle down sometime, and for the most part, she's alright."

(*What?*) Seth couldn't believe what he was hearing. Seth had wanted to give Mel the benefit of the doubt for Renée's sake, but it just wasn't happening. As much as he believed that people could change, he knew Mel hadn't. He was still the same guy he had known years before. He got an uneasy feeling in his stomach. Although he didn't know Renée very well, he knew Mel. He wanted to believe that Mel had changed since the last time their paths had crossed, but he knew deep in his heart that he hadn't. He was still the same old Mel, always looking out for number one.

Seth uncomfortably looked around. He tried to think of something with which to change the subject, but to no avail as Mel continued. "Yeah, I'm trying to talk Renée into eloping to Las Vegas. I figure that way the wedding would be a quick one, and once we got that formality out of the way, there would be a lot more time to party and gamble. What do you think?"

"I guess," Seth said shrugging his shoulders. He really didn't know what to say.

Mel started to laugh and then asked, "What's happened to you, man? When I knew you before, you used to be so tough. What's the deal?"

"People change, Mel. People change," Seth said as he walked past him into the house. (*Everyone but you.*)

Seth went up the stairs to find Maggie. After the unnerving conversation he had had with Mel, he was ready to leave. Walking into the larger room, the sitting area, he found Maggie and Renée engaged in conversation.

"Oh, hey, Seth," Maggie said getting up from her chair, "thought you might've gotten lost. We were just talking about how Mel and Renée met. It's quite the story."

"Really?" Seth inquired. (*I bet it is*, he wanted to say but didn't.)

"Yeah," Maggie proceeded, "it was at a shopping mall."

"What did Mel get picked up for shoplifting or something?" Seth tried to make it sound light and funny, but from the surprised look on Renée's face, he knew he hadn't succeeded.

"No, no," Maggie continued, oblivious to the undertone in Seth's remark, "it was actually in the parking lot. Mel had a flat tire, and he didn't know how to change it. So Renée changed it for him."

"So you were there to rescue him?" Seth looked deeply into Renée's eyes.

Renée gave him a puzzled look. "I guess. I never really thought of it that way."

"But isn't that kind of funny?" Maggie pressed on with the conversation. "I mean, usually it's the guy that helps the girl not vice versa. Honestly, Renée, I wouldn't even know the first thing about using a jack or anything. How did you learn that stuff?"

"I like cars," Renée answered, but she was still feeling uncomfortable under Seth's gaze. She was thinking about the comment he had just made.

# Chapter II

"What? Do you want to turn this into a God-damned boarding house? What the hell is your problem, Renée? You can't help every homeless bastard in this world," Mel said as he blew smoke into the air from his cigarette. He and Renee were sitting on the deck of their house. It was only May, and Renée was already feeling like buying the house was one of the biggest mistakes she had ever made. As with a lot of decisions, she had felt pressured by Mel into purchasing it. Mel had said something like 'Friends of my dad's,' 'We could get a good deal,' and 'Don't you want to live here with me and raise a family?' Renée tiredly looked at Mel. She worked as the Youth Activity Director at the local YMCA, and on her salary alone, they would not be able to pay the mortgage. Mel had been working as a cook at a local restaurant, but to Renée's dismay, he had, without warning, abruptly quit his job. She would not have been so upset, if this had been the first job he had quit without warning. Prior to this one, he had been working at a woodworking shop. When he had decided that job was not the right fit, he had just decided one morning not to get up and go to work. Renée had been beside herself. The mortgage had been coming due, and there had not been enough money to cover it. At about the same time, Maggie needed a place to stay which truly had been a blessing. Although Renée had not asked, Maggie had insisted that she pay something for rent. About two weeks had passed after quitting at the woodworking shop, and Mel's dad had told him about a job as a cook. He (his dad) knew the owner, and Mel would be able to begin immediately. But after working for about a week and a half, Mel again decided it was not the right fit. Because of this, Renée had proposed to him the idea of renting another room, like they had been doing with Maggie, until their financial situation got better.

"Mel," Renée gently said, choosing her words carefully, "I realize the job market isn't the greatest right now, and I know in time you'll get a job, but until then, this will help us pay our bills."

"What?" he asked standing up as he contemptuously glared at her. "Now, you're saying I'm a bum because I don't have a job?" He dramatically threw his arms in the air over his head. "Whatever, Renée, do what you want. Rent out rooms to everyone in the whole God-damned country if you want. You always do what you want."

She couldn't help the tears that sprung to her eyes. "I didn't mean it like that," she added quietly.

"Oh, poor, poor Renée, now the waterworks start. Whatever. You're gonna do what you want. If we need money so badly, why don't you ask my dad? You know he's loaded. I wouldn't even *have* to work. He'll support us."

"Mel, we can't rely on your dad for *everything*," Renée stated with frustration. She took a deep breath and did her best to calm herself. Trying to keep her voice steady, she continued, "Yes, he has helped us out a lot, but if we're ever going to have a life together, we really need to start doing things on our own."

"Just because your family doesn't give a rat's ass about you doesn't mean that my old man won't be there for us," he remarked as he finally sat back down beside her.

"That's not true. My family does care, Mel, but. . ."

"They just don't like me. They think you're too good for me, that I'm bringing you down," Mel complained in a mimicking tone. He angrily turned towards her and haughtily explained, "Well, I got news for you, Renée, you would be nothing without me. Do you hear me? Nothing. It was my dad who got the deal to go through for this house. You better get it through that thick head of yours that if I ever left you, you'd never make it." As his voice rose filled with anger and frustration, he added, "Do you hear me?"

"Yes." Renée sadly nodded as she somberly turned away. Seeing some weeds in the small flowerbed by the deck, she got up and half-heartedly began pulling them out by their roots.

Unfortunately for Mel, he was right about the fact that her family didn't like him. Renée had gone round and round with her dad about the importance of accepting Mel, but her dad would have no part of it and had plainly told her, "He's no good for you. If you stay with him, all he's going to do is bring you down. Why can't you see that? Why can't you see what's so clear to everyone else?"

Renée had ignored his words of wisdom. Now when she needed her family the most, she felt as if she could not turn to them for help. The line between them had been clearly drawn. Renée's pride would not allow her to admit that they had been right all along, and fear of what Mel would ever do if she tried to leave him hung over her like a dark, ominous fog. She couldn't see where the future would lead, and she couldn't see back to from where she had come. She felt like she was stuck in the same place, day after day, covering the same ground, getting nowhere.

"Now come here," he said as he patted the space beside

him. His voice had suddenly gone from upset and argumentative to soft and gentle. "Come sit with me so we can talk."

Leaving the gardening for later, she begrudgingly sat beside him and stared into his blue eyes. She so wanted to believe that things would be okay that he would prove to everyone that he could be the man that she believed he could be. That for once her family would accept him, and that they too would see the goodness, although flawed at times, that she saw in him.

He wrapped his arm around her shoulders, kissed the top of her head, and soothingly asked, "Would it really help finances that much if we had another person living here for a while?" He turned to Renée and asked, "You realize this would only be temporary just like with Maggie?"

"Yes," she calmly replied as she waited for him to continue.

"Okay, but two is all. Do you understand?" Mel asked authoritatively. "Maggie already has the upstairs room, and Seth could stay in the downstairs room for awhile. But, as with Maggie, Seth has to understand that there are some rules." Mel stretched out his arms in front of him, as he cracked his knuckles. "Mainly that the main floor is mine, and he really has no business hanging out there."

"Alright," Renée said without question, "I'll explain it to him. I'm sure he'll have no problems with that."

"And his ex- what's her name? Kathy? Well, she has no business coming around here. You and I both know why." Renée gave him a puzzled look. "Well, Renée, isn't it obvious? Have you not met her? You know she has a thing for me," he said as he smiled conceitedly.

"Oh, I didn't know. . ." Renée trailed off.

"Of course you didn't," Mel said with obvious annoyance as he flicked his finished cigarette into the backyard. "You're too dumb sometimes to figure these things out. You have no idea, do you? Do you realize how many women there are out there that would love to be in your position? I've had a lot of women who wanted to marry me, but for some reason, I settled for you." Renée sadly turned away. "Oh, I didn't mean it that way, honey," Mel said as he grabbed her and held her closely and whispered, "I just sometimes don't think you realize how lucky you are to have me. Come on Renée, even though you'd like to believe it, your family really doesn't care that much about you. You know this don't you? So you really need to start understanding, honey, that I am *your* family. Yes, we might have some tough times, and things aren't perfect all the time, but we do have a great life together. Don't you agree?"

Renée just looked up at him and pleadingly asked, "Mel, *will* you be getting a job soon?"

He smiled a sappy smile and took her hands in his. "Honey, that is so weird! I was just going to bring that up. Earlier, I felt attacked by you, and I completely forgot about my news until now. Now that I've relaxed because you aren't on my back about everything, I'll tell you." His tone almost sounded repentant as he continued, "I'm so sorry that I haven't been pulling my weight lately, but I'm gonna make it up to you, okay? See there's this guy that I know who's starting this contracting business, and he needs a supervisor. It'll be easy money, great pay. Although you sometimes get so caught up with helping others out, soon we won't have to have any tenants. You could even quit that crummy job that you have playing with the kids, and you wouldn't have to work." He beamed proudly as he lit another cigarette.

"It's not a crummy job, I'm the Youth Director, and I love working there. Why do you always have to put my work down?"

"Yeah, whatever," he said obviously uninterested in what she was saying. As he exhaled, he questioned with annoyance, "Do you want to hear about my new job or what?" He looked at Renée. Before she had a chance to answer, he continued, "Okay, I'll be- get this- telling people where to go and what to do all day. The way Roger explained it, all I have to do is get to know a few things about the business, and I'll be good to go."

Renée looked puzzled. "But what exactly will you be doing?"

"Oh, it's an out of the home business, selling products to people in need of them. Customers will contact me, and I'll contract out services. Don't you get it? Are you that simple, baby?"

But Renée didn't get it. She had an uneasy feeling about his new job, and an even more uneasy feeling about Roger. She remembered him from the restaurant at which Mel had worked. Each time she had come in to talk to Mel, Roger had given her the creeps. There was no other way to describe him but as a lazy slime ball who was always looking for the easy way out. She wanted to ask Mel more about what kind of business he and Roger would be running, but the phone rang.

"I'll get it," Mel answered as he stood up. "I'm sure it's for me anyway." He went inside. She was still thinking about Mel's job when she heard him rudely say, "Hello. Yeah, she's here. What do you want? Oh, yeah, yeah, I forgot man. Yeah. No worries. That'll work. Okay, I'll see you then."

Mel came back outside and handed her the phone saying, "It's your boyfriend."

"What?" Renée gave him a puzzled look.

"Yeah, it's Seth," he said with a smirk. "I'm going over to Roger's. We have some business to talk about. I'll be back later."

She covered the receiver and asked, "What time?" But he was already in his car backing out of the driveway.

Seth nervously waited for Renee's voice to come over the line. What was he thinking? Considering how he felt about her, was it really a good idea to rent a room from her and Mel? Part of him wanted to, because although he hadn't known her for very long, he felt a need to be close to her. As bizarre as it sounded, even to him, he wanted to be there to protect her- from exactly what he was not entirely sure. He had an unexplainable feeling about it. From past experiences, he had learned to trust his gut instinct. He was tired. He had spent the majority of the day packing his things at his and Kathy's old apartment. Initially, she had said that she would stay at her mom's until the end of the month, and that Seth could stay at the apartment. But out of the blue which Seth still couldn't believe would surprise him, she had called and said she had changed her mind. So he had to be the one to move. She had proceeded to tell him that if he did not comply with her wishes, she would go straight down to the court house and file a restraining order.

"A what?" he had asked in disbelief. "On what grounds?"

"Oh, I'll think of something," she had stated matter-of-fact. "You know I will."

Instead of arguing a moot point, he had agreed to leave. In view of the fact that it was the middle of the month, he really didn't know where he could go on such short notice. That was when he had thought of Renée. He had nervously dialed Renee's number; the one Maggie had given him in case he needed to get a hold of her, and had talked to Renée. To Seth's surprise, she had said she did not see why he couldn't stay there for a while, but she would have to ask Mel.

"Of course," Seth had responded. What he had wanted to say was far different from that two word statement. Although he had not known Renée for very long, he was very touched by her kindness and sincerity. (*Women like her are few and far between.*) He also had to remind himself that staying with them was temporary, and that it would be in his best interest not to get involved in her and Mel's relationship. He knew he was kidding himself, for the feeling he felt when he had first met her would not go away. He had a knowing deep inside him that something, although he wasn't certain exactly what, was going to happen. But, for the time being, he had to be reminiscent of the fact that she was engaged to Mel. A relationship he off-handedly referred to as the *Beauty and the Beast.*

"Hello? Hello?" Seth had been so lost in thought that the sound of Renée's voice almost startled him as he was jerked back to reality.

"Oh, hi, Renée. Sorry about that. It's been a long day."

"Oh, I'm sorry to hear that." She paused briefly and then said, "I did talk to Mel, and he agreed that it would be okay if you stay here for awhile." (*Barely,* she thought recalling the conversation she had had with Mel.)

"Yeah? Hey, I really appreciate this." He continued nervously, "I realize this is so last minute, but honestly, I didn't know what to do."

"I understand." She took a breath and continued, "I know what it's like when you're in a situation, and you really don't have anywhere to go or anyone to turn to."

(*I bet you do*, Seth wanted to say.) He casually asked, "So, when can I move my things in? I don't have very much. I put most of it in storage and the rest, well, that's another story. . ." (*Yeah*, thought Seth as he let the thought trail off.) Kathy had kindly offered to keep most of his things. Because he was sick and tired of arguing and listening to her rant and rave, he had just walked away.

"Oh." Renée sounded confused as if she didn't know how to respond. "I guess," she continued slowly, "sometimes those things happen. But as far as moving in, I imagine you don't have a place to stay for right now. So unless you're planning on sleeping in your car, a tent, or renting a room for the night, you're welcome to come over right now. Maggie didn't sound like she had any plans after her shift, so she'll probably be around if you need some help. And Mel, well, he went out for the evening. He said he had some business to discuss." She still got that uneasy feeling in her stomach when she thought of Roger and the new business venture. Trying to dismiss that from her mind, she added, "And of course I'm here too."

"Okay," Seth replied. "Are you hungry? Do you want me to stop and get a pizza or something?"

"Actually," Renée said as she felt her stomach growl, "that'd be great. To be honest, I kind of lost track of time. Initially Mel and I had plans to go out and eat, but well. . ."

"Alright." He paused slightly, awkwardly wondering if he should say something. But if he did, that would be considered getting involved. Instead he said, "I'll be to your house before the sun sets. Any special kind of pizza?"

"Anything but pepperoni," Renée said and walked in the house to hang up the phone.

After the conversation with Seth, Renée opened the front door. She sat in her favorite spot on the steps which she had nicknamed *The Stoop*. It was three concrete steps that led to the front yard. In the flowerbeds on each side of it, she had planted irises. She adored the purple flowers that had started to bloom. She looked up at the tall evergreen tree about twenty feet to the left of the stoop. She loved that tree. It was old, standing the test of time. It was unwavering and strong, qualities for which she desperately longed. "I wonder what that tree could say if it'd talk. I wonder what tales it could tell," Renée said quietly. She stared blankly up at the tree. She thought of Mel. (*What am I going to do?*) She looked to the west and observed the amazingly breathtaking sight of the sun beginning to set. Orange and red hues were stretching across the sky. She let out a sigh as she began quietly whispering into the warm air, "God, I know you're there, and I really need You." She brushed away a tear that was sliding down her cheek. "I know I don't always live my life exactly how You would probably have me, and I know I make a lot of mistakes, but I'm still asking for Your help. Send me something, God. Something so I know You haven't forgotten about me." Renée closed her eyes and sat quietly meditating on the solitude until a rumbling brought her back to reality. She opened her eyes and looked around her. Then she realized the noise was coming from the driveway. She stood up, walked around the side of the house, and there she saw the most amazing sight. In the driveway was parked a metallic blue 1969 Chevy Camaro seemingly illuminated by the color changes still present in the sky. Renée's mouth dropped in amazement when the door opened, and Seth got out of the driver's seat.

"Pizza anyone?" he asked with a smile.

Renée didn't know what to say. She looked from Seth, to the car, and back to Seth again.

"Uh, Renée?" Seth asked confused as he shut the door of the car. Pizza in hand, he walked towards her. "Are you okay?"

"Yes!" Renée exclaimed a little too enthusiastically. "Oh," she apologized embarrassedly, "I didn't mean to stare. It's just that . . . it's just that . . .," she stammered, "that's my dream car, and I can't believe *you* are driving it!" Renée walked closer to the car and looked up at Seth quizzically. "Do you care if I *touch* it?"

"Renée," he smiled and dangled the keys from his fingers, "do you want to *drive* her?"

Renée was so surprised that she almost didn't catch the keys when Seth tossed them to her. She looked from Seth to the car and back at Seth again. "Are you serious?" she exclaimed, almost waiting for him to change his mind.

"Hop in," he said holding open the driver's door. "If you don't mind cold pizza, I could set this in the house while we take her for a spin." Renée stared dumb-founded as she watched Seth walk up the steps, open the door, and go into the house. When he came out, he gave her a strange look. "Well, what're you waiting for? Get in!"

"Oh, right," Renée said glancing at the driver's door that was still open. "But, are you positive about this?"

Seth scratched his head and looked at Renée. "Is there any reason I shouldn't trust you?"

"Well, no."

"Then," Seth said getting in the passenger side and rolling down the window so he could talk to her, "come on! I really would like to get my things unpacked before it gets too dark."

Renée gingerly got in the seat, grasped the steering wheel, and looked around at the interior. It was just as clean and meticulously kept as the outside. It was the most beautiful car in which she had ever been. Adjusting her seat and the mirrors, she put her seat belt on, and started the engine. "Man alive! I can't believe I'm actually going to drive this!" She turned to Seth. "Seth, I don't know how to thank you, but I'm never going to forget this!"

"Renée, it's not that big of a deal."

"It is to me! You have no idea how long I've wanted to drive a car like this! She's definitely a beauty."

"Princess," Seth said quietly, a hint of embarrassment spreading across his face as he grinned boyishly.

"Huh?"

"Her name is Princess. I got her when I was fourteen." He laughed nervously. "She was my first real love." Seth fastened his seatbelt, turned to Renée and continued,

"I was too young to drive, but my dad and I were going to fix her up. You know a father and son thing."

"From the looks of this car, that went well. Right?" Renée briefly glanced at Seth as she smoothly slid the car into reverse and began backing out of the driveway. "Or not?" She added observing the expression on Seth's face.

"Well," Seth answered as he looked out the passenger window, "the important thing is that she *did* get restored."

\* \* \*

Seth remembered it like it was yesterday. His dad had bought Princess at a junkyard, and she had been in pretty tough shape. As his dad had driven her into the yard, she had sputtered and shaken. Seth's mom had looked out the kitchen window and had smiled. "Good, he listened to me," she had said quietly. Seth's mom had suggested to his dad that the two of them work on something together- build something or fix something, anything that would get them to work side by side. She had been concerned about the two of them not getting along, and she had hoped some kind of project would change this.

"Dad!" Seth had exclaimed slamming the front door as he had almost fallen down the front steps before asking, "Where'd you get this?" He had not even been the least bit bothered by the knocking and banging noises the car had been emitting.

His dad had gone onto explain how he had purchased the car at the local junkyard, and how he had thought he and Seth could work on restoring it. "It'll take a lot of work, but as long as you do what I say, we'll be able to get her running," his dad had remarked. His eyes had shown that he already had in mind what the finished product would look like, as he was very stubborn and accustomed to doing things his way.

Unfortunately, Seth and his dad had only gotten some of the work on the engine finished when they had gotten into a big fight. "If you think you are so God-damned good with cars, then do it yourself!" his dad had screamed after slamming a wrench against the side panel. "As you know, I *do* have a bit of experience. Maybe if you wouldn't be on such a high horse, you could benefit from it."

"Dad," Seth had looked at his dad with a challenging gaze, "I *never* said you weren't good with cars. I just had an idea. I didn't say we had to do it."

"Don't you talk back to me!" his dad had screamed raising his hand. Seth had flinched, expecting to be at the other end of his dad's fist. Instead his dad had thrown down the wrench, walked out of the shop, talking under his breath as he left, but loud enough so Seth could hear him, "No good kid. He never does anything right, and there's no way in hell he's going to do anything right with that car." Seth and his dad's relationship had always been a strained one, and that insult had been the pivotal point in which Seth had made a conscious decision to exclude his dad from anything important in his life.

After that belittling altercation, Seth had made a commitment to himself to get Princess restored to a greater beauty than she even had been in her prime. He had gotten every car magazine possible, and although he normally wasn't much for studying, he had spent hours upon hours reading and learning everything he could. When he had a question, he had gone to a guy he had known named Carl at a local mechanic shop. He had helped him out as much as possible. Even with all the help, it still hadn't been enough. A car like Princess had needed a lot of parts, a paint job, a new exhaust, and so much more. Seth had known that things like that would cost a lot of money. So eventually, after not too much convincing, Carl had offered Seth a job at his garage. Seth couldn't believe that the tables had finally turned in his favor, but unfortunately, this had only been temporary. At Carl's garage, car engines, exhausts and repairs had not been the only things with which his employees had been interested. At Carl's garage, Seth had taken his first hit from a joint.

* * *

Letting the image go as he brought himself back to reality, Seth realized Renée was asking him a question. "So, Seth, how fast *does* this car go?"

Smiling, Seth adjusted his seatbelt more tightly, and turned his attention to Renée. "I guess you'll have to find out."

Renée stepped on the accelerator as they got on the freeway. She easily shifted gears as the car picked up more and more speed. She was passing cars effortlessly when Seth leaned over in an attempt to get a glimpse of the speedometer and asked, "How fast *are* you going?"

Renée shot him a quick smile. "I know, I know. I'll slow it down." No sooner than she slowed down to the posted speed limit, Renée and Seth saw red flashing lights. A car was pulled over on the shoulder of the freeway.

"Huh," Seth said turning around and waving to the man rolling down his window, so he could give his driver's license and proof of registration to the officer. "You're so lucky!"

"You think so?" Renée questioned, stifling a laugh while exiting from the freeway. "Maybe I'm just blessed because of your company."

Seth started laughing. "Sure, sure, whatever you say."

"Wow, this is quite the car. If you ever want to sell her, make sure you keep me in mind."

"Never," Seth said. "She's one lady that's definitely worth holding onto. And at least with her, what you see is what you get. I know her so well that there're no surprises, and I like that. You know, a lot of cars made today are beautiful on the outside, but their engines need a major overhaul. I like classic cars- what you see is what you get."

Renée looked at Seth and shook her head. "You know, Seth, if I didn't know better, I'd ask you if you were referring to women instead of cars."

Seth thought about that statement for a while. "Well, maybe that's a good philosophy to have with both."

"Interesting," Renée said as she turned on a side street that would take them back to her house.

They drove by a few bars. Renée slowed down and

sadly looked out the window.

"What?" Seth asked wondering at what she was looking. Confused by her expression, he offered, "Did you want to stop for a drink?"

"No," Renée replied unhappily. "No, it's just that . . . Oh, what does it matter?"

Seth turned around in his seat, glanced out the window, and saw what he believed to be Mel's car parked in front of one of the local hangouts. "Oh," he said turning and facing forward. Again he felt the urge to say *something* to Renée so she would realize what a pathetic loser Mel was, but he had a sneaking suspicion that it was not anything that she did not already know. (*It probably wouldn't do much good anyway.*) He sat quietly sticking to his resolve of not getting involved.

"You know, Seth, you don't know Mel like I do." She took a deep breath and wondered why she always felt the need to defend him. Why she always felt it was her duty to get others to see the side of him with which she had fallen in love.

"You're right, Renée, I don't."

She quickly glanced over at Seth, opened her mouth slightly as if she were going to speak, but instead tried to keep a tear from falling down her cheek. When she regained her composure, she said, "He didn't drink at all when we first met. In the past couple of months, he has changed so much. It's like he's a different person." She nervously moved her hands up and down the sides of the steering wheel. "I know that sounds so cliché, but it's the truth." She grasped the steering wheel tightly as she slowed down for a stop sign. "I don't know why I'm telling you this, Seth, as if you need to hear about the crap that's going on in my life."

"Renée," Seth said turning his gaze towards her, "believe me, I'm the last person in the world who is in a position to judge anyone else's relationship." He slightly laughed. "Or haven't you figured it out yet that I don't exactly have the best track record?"

Renée turned to him and smiled. "Really? I figured you were some big Casanova who travels around the country breaking hearts as you go."

"No," Seth said smiling at her comment. "No, Renée, I'm not. On the contrary; I'm usually the one who gets his heart broken. It's a curse I guess."

"What's a curse?" Renée curiously asked.

"Falling for women who I think I love because I can see all the potential and good in them. I can see the person I believe they could become." Seth took a deep breath in, let it out, and quickly glanced out the window. "Now I'm the one who feels awkward at saying too much."

Keeping her eyes on the road, Renée didn't say anything for awhile. Finally, she asked, "So you think I'm believing, hoping, dreaming of something that's never going to be?"

Seth let his head drop back on the headrest. He carefully chose his words. "Renée, there's no one in the world who can answer that question expect you."

Renée didn't want to admit it, but she knew Seth was right.

When Seth and Renée returned from their drive, Maggie was sitting on the steps while animatedly talking on her cell phone. She waved to them, as she said her goodbyes and hung up the phone. "Hi, hi, good news, good news!" She stood up and twisted from side to side, then looked more carefully at Renée and Seth. "Hey, Renée, were you driving Seth's car? You were. Weren't you?" She turned to Seth. "Seth, I've known you a lot longer than you've known Renée, and you've never let me drive Princess! What gives?"

"I don't know Maggie, maybe because I trust Renée." Seth laughed and then added, "For two reasons Mags. One,

I've seen how you drive, and I want to keep her around for a little while longer; and two, you've *never* asked!"

"Oh," Maggie said ignoring the first part of the statement. "I guess maybe some time I'll have to." She put her hands on the square of her back. "Ah, my back's been bugging me."

"Anyway," Seth questioned, "*that* is the good news?"

"Oh, no, no, no," she laughed. "No, I just got off the phone with Joe."

"So *that's* the good news?" Renée butted in.

"No!" Maggie said stomping her foot. "No, now stop it you two!" Seth and Renée looked at each other and could not help but to laugh at Maggie's childlike response to their teasing.

"Okay, we're sorry. What is it, Mags?" Seth earnestly asked.

"Okay, get this: Joe is going to open a bar and grill, a little restaurant! He just got approved for the loan, and he just got back from checking out a prime location that just went up for sale! Isn't this exciting? What do you guys think?"

"Yeah," Seth agreed. "Sounds really good. Is this something he's wanted to do for a while?"

"Yes," Maggie said as she took a sip from her water bottle. "It's been a dream of his for as long as I've known him, so that's been a while. He always says that he's sick of the "gut bombs" most of those places serve, and he wants a more "home-style" place where people can come and hang out and eat good food. You know, just have a good time."

"That sounds really, really good," said Renée. "There are a lot of restaurants but most of them are either college hangouts, dives, or the food is just raunchy. I'm excited for him. What do you think he'll name the place?"

Maggie rolled her eyes. "He wants to call it *Joe's Place*. That's it, nothing else. Pretty exciting, wouldn't you agree?"

Seth just smiled. "Sounds like he's keeping it pretty simple, and I kind of like the idea- Joe's Place- yeah, it's got a nice down to earth ring to it. If the name's any way to gauge the success of the place, then well, I think he'll do all right."

"Glad *you* think so. I think it's kind of corny myself. I think he should call it . . . uh, uh . . . oh, I don't know! But hey, whatever makes him happy," Maggie commented. Already finished with the conversation, she sat back down on the steps, picked up the paper that she had been paging through and said, "Hum, this looks like a good time."

"What?" Renée said pulling down the page, so she could see at what Maggie was looking.

"There's going to be a hot air balloon at the fair grounds this weekend." Maggie looked at Seth and Renée, her eyes growing wider. "Doesn't that sound fun?"

"Oh, that would be fun," Renée said looking at the paper with Maggie. "How much do you think it'll cost? Maybe Mel would want to go too."

Maggie looked more carefully at the ad. "It doesn't say. But anyway, it can't be too much. Do you guys want to go?"

"Yeah, that would be alright," Seth nodded in agreement, "but it'd have to be after soccer practice. Would that be okay?"

"Fine by me." Maggie shrugged as she folded the paper and set it down beside her on the steps.

Renée looked inquisitively at Seth. "You play soccer?"

"No, no," Seth said holding onto the rail of the steps. "No, I help out with the Saturday Youth Soccer Program. I never really played the game until I started volunteering. It's fun. A great way to get out of yourself and give something back, you know?"

"Hmmmm," Renée smiled, "it does sound like fun."

"Do you want to come with me? There's always room for more volunteers."

"Ah, I don't know. It's been years since I've played, so the kids will probably laugh at me."

"Naw, they're just little rug rats. They're just out there to have a good time. It's nothing too serious."

Renée thought about it. "Okay, yeah, I'll go with you as long as I've your word that no one is going to laugh at me."

"And if someone does, would that really be such a terrible thing?" he teased as he looked into Renée's smiling brown eyes.

"Uh," Renée said feeling her cheeks getting red from Seth's gaze, and she desperately wanted to change the subject, "there's still pizza in the house that's getting cold. I don't know about the two of you, but I'm really hungry."

"Not me," Maggie said licking her lips. "I already helped myself to a couple pieces, and they were mmmm, mmmm good!" Then she added seriously, "You guys don't mind, do you?"

"No," Seth said laughing at Maggie's impersonation of a Campbell's Soup kid. "No, Maggie, I don't mind, but you do know what this means, don't you?"

Maggie shot him a puzzled look, but Renée caught on to where the conversation was leading. "It means," Renée chimed in, "that now you get to help with the unloading of Seth's things. Seth brought the pizza over to entice me to let him stay in the basement for awhile."

"Oh, that'll be way cool!" Maggie got to her feet. "I mean you staying here, not me helping you unload your things. Do I really have to?" she whined like a child. "I'm sooooooooooo tired!"

"Tough," Seth said, "that was the deal. Now come on."

Renée could not help but to laugh when Maggie stuck her tongue out at Seth. She then extended her arm and said to Renée, "Okay, help me to my feet."

# Chapter III

Renée, Seth, and Maggie, in spite of her constant complaining about her *aching back,* carried in Seth's things and set them in his room in the basement. As he had previously told Renée, he did not bring a lot with him, so it did not take too long to get him situated. The room was small but comfortable. Seth did not mind; it was a place to sleep, and he did not need a lot. He looked around at the neatly made bed, the brown, wooden dresser on which he had set a few of his possessions, and the old, worn out blue chair on which lay a few matching pillows. (*So*, he thought contentedly, *this is my home for awhile.*) By the bed was a small nightstand on which sat a small lamp which he could use to read at night. "Perfect," he said with a smile.

Unpacking the few items he had brought with him for the temporary stay, he came across a picture of Kathy. He stared at it trying to remember what he was ever thinking by getting into a relationship with her. She was pretty, very pretty, on the outside anyway. She had long blonde hair, blue eyes, and a figure that would definitely stop traffic.

But her beauty did not extend beyond her exterior appearance. She had a shallow, self-centered way about her. One to which Seth had been blinded. Initially when he had met her, he had trusted her to be sincere. "It's no one's fault but my own," he admitted while crumbling up her picture and throwing it into the garbage. "I'm the one who got involved with her."

Then his thoughts went to Renée- how different she was from Kathy. He knew it was unfair to compare the two and not in the least bit productive. Experiencing first hand Renée's generosity and sincerity made it difficult not to wonder why there were not more women like her in the world and less women like Kathy. He concluded that, to that question, he probably would never know the answer. So instead of reminiscing about a failed relationship, he went upstairs to join Renée and Maggie in eating some pizza. (*That's if there's any left*, he thought emitting a slight laugh as he scratched his head wondering how Maggie could stay so thin considering how much she always ate.)

Seth, Maggie, and Renée were sitting at the table in the dining room talking when they heard a loud blare from a car horn. Renée got up and went to find out what was going on. Reaching for the doorknob, she was almost knocked over as the door slammed open from the outside.

In stumbled Mel, obviously drunk, and extremely annoyed. "Do you mind telling me whose piece of crap car's parked in my spot?" he yelled at Renée.

Overcome with embarrassment, Renée desperately tried to calm him by saying in a hushed voice, "Mel, Seth and Maggie are in the other room. Could you please keep it down?" Then trying to change the subject she added, "How'd the meeting go with Roger?"

"Fine, just fine," he said slurring slightly. "We had a few beers after our meeting."

(*And you drove home in this state you're in?* Renée thought as she gently shut the door.)

Mel staggered into the kitchen, leaned against the counter, and irritatingly spat out, "I'm gonna ask one more time, and I'm trying hard not to get mad. *Who* parked in *my* spot?"

"Sorry, man," Seth said getting up from the table, "I didn't know there was assigned parking."

"Oh, wise guy," Mel hissed as he walked unsteadily to the table towards Seth. "Well, apparently you idiot, you don't know a lot about what goes on around here, do you?"

"Hey, it's no big deal. I'll move it," Seth said in a calm voice unbeknownst to the irritation and annoyance he was feeling. (*What a punk ass*, he said to himself.)

"You're damned right you will! Don't ever park there again, or else you're going to have to deal with me!" Mel yelled flexing his muscles at Seth.

"Okay, okay, just let it go," Seth said getting annoyed as he walked past Mel. It took everything in Seth's power not to turn around and slug him.

Mel looked at Renée, who looked as if she was going to cry. "What? What's the matter with you? You know that's my spot. If he's gonna stay here, he's gotta realize there're certain rules that need to be followed."

"Okay," Renée concluded quietly. She took a deep breath and gently coaxed, "Now, Mel, maybe it's time for you to call it a night. Why don't you get ready for bed?"

Mel glared at Renée. "I will when I damn well feel like it. Since when do *you* think you can tell *me* what to do?" He sat down at the table next to Maggie, ignoring Renée as if the altercation between them had never occurred, leaned in, and said with a twisted grin, "Hi Maggie, how're you doin'?"

"Fine," Maggie said as she noisily moved her chair away from him. Out of respect for Renée, she held back what she really wanted to say. Instead, she asked in an exasperated tone, biting off each word, "Want some pizza, Mel?" She shoved the box towards him and added with impatience, "Maybe some food will help sober you up."

Mel let out a slight laugh. "Ha, I'm not even that drunk. It's just that dumb-asses like wise guy there really get on my nerves." He looked at Maggie, giving her the once over, and then added with a loose smile, "You know Maggie, I'm a pretty amazing guy once you get to know me."

"Whatever," Maggie said agitatedly as she noisily stood up and walked to where Renée was standing. Arms crossed in front of her, she mumbled. "I wouldn't want to get to know you."

Mel remained seated in his chair, his arm draped over the back with an expression of surprised rejection. He clumsily grabbed a piece of pizza and started eating. Finally, after realizing that his obvious attempt at winning Maggie over had failed, he pathetically turned his attention to Renée. "Hey, Renée, honey, I'm sorry," he spoke in a sorrowful voice while rudely talking with a mouthful of pizza. "It's just that you know I want things the way I want them." He finished his pizza, wiped his mouth on his shirt, got up from the table, and walked to the bedroom. "I'm going to bed."

Renée stood by the sink in the kitchen staring out the window. Maggie remained by her side, arms still tightly crossed in front of her. Lately, Mel's drinking had gotten worse and worse. Renée rubbed the back of her neck trying to remember why she had fallen in love with Mel in the first place. She remembered the first days when they had been dating, so much had changed since that time. (*And now what? Would things ever go back to the way they had been, or would they continue to get progressively worse?*) She felt so alone, so uncertain of what the future would hold. She took in a deep breath and let it out. (*Maybe it's something I'm doing wrong. Maybe I nag too much or expect too much.*) She was not oblivious to the fact that all relationships have their ups and downs, but lately, there seemed to be more downs than ups.

Renée heard the door open and close, and she turned to see Seth facing her. "I'm really sorry, Seth. He gets like that sometimes when he has had too much to drink," she stated apologetically. She looked down, not daring to look into Seth's eyes.

"Hey," Seth said gently, lifting her chin, "you're not the one who should be apologizing. You didn't do anything wrong, Renée."

"Then why do I feel like it's always my fault?" she imploringly questioned as tears started to slide down her cheeks.

"Hey," Maggie said uncrossing her arms and gently putting one across Renée's shoulders, "drunks are good at making us feel that way. I should know."

Seth and Renée looked at Maggie.

"I used to be in a relationship with a drunk, and I always felt like it was my fault," Maggie bit her lip. "It took me quite some time to realize it wasn't." Maggie continued with her story. "I had just graduated from high school, wiped the dirt off my feet from the small town I had lived in all my life, and I was headed for the big city. My goal was to become a professional hair dresser for top super models. That sounds so lame! Doesn't it?"

"No," Renée said, wanting Maggie to continue. She smiled. "It's good to have dreams."

"I wanted to prove to everyone back home that I was something special. I wanted it all- all the glory and fame of doing famous people's hair. I started classes at a beauty college, and a friend of a friend introduced me to Mike one night at a party. I didn't have a lot of experience dating. I was young, and I thought I was in love." Maggie laughed lightly, looked up at Renée and Seth waiting for them to laugh at what she thought to be the absurdness of her naïve belief. Surprised that they didn't, she went on. "He said all the right things, did all the right things, and ultimately, I fell head over heels for him. At first it was great, or at least I thought so. I wasn't old enough to buy alcohol, and he was. Life turned into one big party. He started drinking more and more. The more he drank, the more controlling he became. I tried to break up with him, but whenever I did, he would come back so sorry for what he had done. He would always have a new resolve to quit drinking for good. The promises he made, although I believe he was sincere when he made them, usually lasted for no longer than a couple of days. Then he would show up at my place drunk, again. Not knowing any better at the time, and always believing he would change, I kept taking him back. Without realizing it, each time I did, he took any serenity and peace that I had in my life.

"As if the drinking and controlling behavior weren't bad enough, he started becoming really abusive. At first it started with him pushing me around. Honestly, at the time, I didn't take it too seriously. But then the pushing and shoving escalated to slapping me across the face and grabbing me by the hair like he was a Neanderthal man or something. After that, I had enough. I wanted out. It wasn't easy, but finally after a lot of counseling, completely distancing myself from him, and learning to take care of myself, I was able to break free from the unhealthy hold he had over me. I was more in love with the idea of being in love than in love itself, if that makes any sense.

"It wasn't easy, but I did move on. After almost becoming a beauty school drop out, I talked with my instructors, and I was completely honest with them about what had happened. I was put on academic probation instead of getting kicked out. Well, to make a long story short, I worked my butt off, finished my degree, did my practicum, and after applying for a million different jobs, I finally got a break. I landed a job at a well known salon only on a temporary basis until I proved myself. Fortunately, for me, it didn't take me too long to build up my clientele. Hey, I may not be doing hair for professional models or actresses or anything, but I enjoy my job and I'm damn good at what I do."

Renee looked at Maggie for a few moments after she had finished speaking, and then looking down she quietly remarked, "That's quite the story." Renée's arms were still protectively crossed in front of her as she shifted uneasily not daring to look up from the spot at which she was staring on the floor. Finally, she raised her head. Tears dried against her cheeks and with a defeated note in her voice, she asked, "How'd you finally decide that it was time to leave him?"

"Believe me," Maggie said looking directly into Renée's eyes, "you'll know. You'll just know."

The next morning, Renée woke up early, took her cup of coffee, and went to sit on *The Stoop*. Alone, she closed her eyes and replayed the events of the night before. (*Why did Mel have to drink so much? Was Maggie right? Maybe I'm enabling him to continue with his behavior. But what am I supposed to do?*) If leaving him would be that easy, she would have done it a long time ago. She contemplated the idea of "being in love with the idea of being in love" as Maggie had made reference.

"Mind if I join you?" Startled, Renée turned around to see Seth standing in the doorway. Coffee cup in hand, he smiled down at her.

"No, no, not at all." Renée inched over, so Seth could sit beside her. "What're you doing up so early?"

"Couldn't sleep," he said sitting down next to her, stretching his legs out in front of him. "You neither?"

"No," she calmly replied taking a sip of coffee, "too much on my mind."

"Hmmmm," Seth said trying to sound casual. In spite of trying to hold onto his noble principle of not getting involved, he knew that his intentions had been laid aside a long time ago. So bracing himself for the inevitable, with a bated breath he caringly asked, "Anything you want to talk about?"

Renée took a deep breath, let it out, and earnestly looked at Seth. With a voice filled with despondency and uncertainty, she finally questioned, "Seth, why do relationships have to be so complicated?"

Seth scratched his head and ran his fingers through his hair that was slightly sticking up in the back. "That's quite the question for this early in the morning," he yawned as he set down his coffee cup and stretched his arms over his head. "I don't really know the answer to that one, Renée, and I don't know that anyone truly does."

"Oh," Renée said as she pulled her blanket closer around her shoulders.

"Are you talking about a romantic relationship between a man and woman or just relationships in general?" Seth already knew the answer, but his attempt was to give Renée an opening to continue talking about what was really on her mind, and it worked.

"Relationships between men and women."

"Well, I have a theory on this." Seth took a sip from his coffee, turned to Renée and asked, "Do you want to hear it?"

"Yes."

"Okay. It's no doubt that so many relationships end in divorce because it's difficult to find two people traveling down the same road at the same time."

Renée gave him a confused look. "I don't quite get it."

"Let me explain. Again, it's important for you to remember that this is my theory. It's just a theory, nothing else." He smiled at Renée, as she attempted to rub the sleep from her eyes, and then again pulled her blanket closely around her shoulders. "I believe that people need to grow in three specific areas: mentally, physically, and spiritually. You with me so far?" Renée nodded. "The physical is obvious, and the mental also encompasses the emotional, you know, how grown up a person is. And the spiritual, well, I'll get to that in a minute. Anyway, some people get married because they're physically attracted to each other. They're on the same physical plane, and they physically enjoy one another's company. This works for a while, but what happens when physical beauty starts to fade? If the relationship is based solely on this, it won't last. Also, two people have to be on the same emotional plane. Too many times men get too caught up in suppressing their feelings, and women get too caught up in trying to express them. This gets to be one big mess. Instead of working through things together, there may be times they turn to others who they may think understand them better, if you get my meaning." Seth stopped, raised his eyebrows to emphasize his point, and then looked at Renée who nodded her head. Then he continued, "It's sad, but unfortunately not too uncommon. I think it's because neither of the people in the relationship is ready to grow in this area. Or maybe one person wants to grow and change, but the other person remains in the same place. If this be the case, then there's only one place this relationship usually leads and that is, sorry to say, to a divorce. Finally, the most important is spiritual progress. If two people are honestly committed to each other, the life they're building together, and the belief that a God of their understanding will help them, then their marriage will succeed. It's my belief that if they're doing their best to live along spiritual lines, they'll do what's best to keep the other two areas of their life in check." He took a long laborious breath, pretended to adjust an imaginary pair of glasses, and in his best *professional* voice said, "Thus, contributing to a long and fulfilling married life together." He let go of his façade, laughed, and genuinely added, "Now, I'm not saying things will always be perfect, but they'll always have something that a lot of other couples lack."

"Which is?" Renée asked.

"Hope," Seth answered. He stopped, took a sip from his coffee, and sat quietly waiting for Renée to respond. When she just sat quietly, he finally turned to her. He was surprised to see tears wet against her cheeks. "Hey," he said soothingly, "I'm sorry, Renée. I didn't mean to upset you with my philosophy about. . ."

"No," Renée said as she frustratingly brushed the tears off her face, "it's not what you said Seth, it's just that. . ." she lightly laughed, "it's just that what you said is so true." She turned to him as she rested her head on her knees that were pulled closely to her chest. "Where do you come up with this stuff?"

Seth shrugged his shoulders and embarrassedly replied, "I don't know. It's just what I think about relationships. Honestly, Renee, I didn't mean to upset you."

"Not a big deal," Renée said watching a squirrel scurry up the large evergreen tree.

"This is a cool spot. Do you sit out here a lot?" Seth asked, deliberately changing the subject.

"Yeah, I nicknamed it *The Stoop*. It's kind of like when I was a little kid and I had my secret spot where I could go, and no one would bother me. I guess kind of like a hiding place. Of course, it's not quite the same, but you get the general idea, right?"

(*Do you feel like you have to hide often*? Seth wondered. But instead, he went another direction with the conversation.) "So," Seth inquired, "when I want to talk with you, and you're not in the house or yard, it's a safe bet that I can find you out here?"

"Uh, huh."

"I'll remember that," he said with a sincere smile.

"Okay then," Renée said abruptly rising to her feet. "Are you still going to soccer practice?"

"Oh, yeah," Seth said looking at his watch. "I almost forgot about that. I guess time does fly when you're having fun."

Renée rolled her eyes and grinned. "That's such a corny statement."

Seth shrugged his shoulders, smiled, but didn't say anything.

"Anyway," Renée continued, "I'm going to tell Mel that I'm going with you, and then I'll get ready. How much time do I have?"

Seth looked up at her. "About fifteen minutes."

Renée got up. As she gently closed the screen door, she looked back at Seth through the lines in the screen and smiled. (*He's definitely something.*)

Mel was sprawled across their large bed. A puddle of drool was forming around his cheek which was pressed against the mattress. Somehow he had worked the sheet off of the corner of it, and the white and red roses inched out from under the sheet looking like they were itching his face. The pillows were all on the floor, and one of Mel's uncovered legs peeked out from under the comforter. Renée sat on the bed next to him and gently stroked his cheek. (*He looks so gentle and kind sleeping, maybe Maggie and Seth are wrong about him. Maybe he'll prove to everyone what a wonderful man he can be.*) "Mel," Renée lightly nudged his shoulder, "Mel, honey, will you wake up?"

"Leave me alone, "Mel said rolling onto his side. "I'm trying to sleep."

"Uh, Mel," Renée said, kneeling on the bed by his side, "Seth's going to coach soccer this morning, and he wants me to go with him. I won't be gone for too long. Do you think you might want to come with us?"

"I said," Mel spat out angrily, swatting at Renée as if she were a pesky fly, "leave me alone!"

"Okay," Renée said as she got off the bed careful not to further disturb Mel's sleep. "I just thought I'd let you know where I was going."

"Like I care," he mumbled rolling onto his side deliberately turning away from her.

Renée took a deep breath, opened her mouth to say something, and then stopped. (*Why do I even try?*) She changed into a light blue sweat-suit that she had taken down from its shelf in the closet. She glanced at her watch, and then headed to the bathroom to brush her teeth and put her hair in a ponytail. She had five minutes until she and Seth were going to leave for practice.

Seth and Renée got in his car and pulled out of the driveway. Seth looked over to where Mel's car was parked. (*What a jerk*, he thought as he remembered the scene Mel had made last night when he had gotten home.) Seth had wanted to slap him across the face and tell him to knock it off with the punk attitude. However, that would have probably gotten him thrown out of the house, and he did, after all, need a place to live until he could find a place of his own. He looked at Renée who was blankly staring out the window. (*Why does she stay with him? She's a smart woman. Why can't she figure out that Mel is nothing but a loser who's going to drag her down?*) He was so preoccupied with his thoughts that he did not realize Renée had asked him a question. "Huh?" he embarrassedly asked turning to her. "I'm sorry Renée, what did you say?"

Renée smiled. "Not a big deal, I was just wondering how you got into coaching soccer."

"I don't know," Seth casually answered shrugging his shoulders. "I like little kids."

"Hmmmmmm. Is that all there's to it?"

Seth slightly laughed as he looked at Renée who had one eyebrow cocked. "Say, that eyebrow thing's a pretty neat trick. How'd you learn to do that?"

She grinned smugly. "Practice. It's something I wanted to learn, so I practiced until I got it. It took me quite some time," she reflected. "I spent hours in front of the mirror holding down one eyebrow while attempting to raise the other. It was quite the sight."

"I bet," Seth commented. Then he added with a smile, "Are you always so *tenacious* about things you want to learn?" He deliberately emphasized the word tenacious.

"That's a nice way to put it. I usually just get called stubborn. But the answer to your question, for the most part, is yes. If something is really important to me, I keep trying; keep working at it until I get it. I just don't like giving up."

"Does that go for relationships, too?" Seth stared straight ahead as he asked the question, worried that he may have been out of line.

Renée played with the strings from the hood of her sweatshirt. Finally, without looking up, she quietly commented, "I guess something like that anyway."

Seth felt a pang of guilt as he glanced at her out of the corner of his eye. It was not his intent to upset her, and although he wanted to continue with the conversation, he knew it would be a better idea to change the subject.

Just as he was thinking of something to say to lighten the mood, Renée said, "Initially, I had asked how you had gotten into coaching soccer."

"Well," Seth replied honestly this time, "it's because it's a good way to give back."

"Give back?" Renée gave him a puzzled look.

"Renée, growing up, I wasn't the greatest kid. I made a lot of poor decisions and with those decisions came consequences. The way I look at life today is a lot different than I had even, say, five years ago. Today, I no longer take things for granted. I used to be a very selfish, self-centered, egotistical jerk who thought I could do anything and get away with it. But for the grace of God, I've learned that the world isn't going to always accommodate me or my actions. Because of this, I've learned that it's not always about what I can get out of life. Instead, it's more about what I can put into it."

"Kind of like you reap what you sow?"

"Yeah, kind of like that I guess. Also there're a lot of kids out there that don't have anyone they can look up to, kind of like a role model or something. I figure that since I was given a second chance, maybe somehow, some way, this'll give a lot of these kids a second chance too."

Renée was going to ask him what kind of trouble into which he had gotten and also what had happened to change him. Unfortunately, she was unable. Just as she was about to begin with her questions, they arrived at the soccer field. Renée could already see young boys and girls gathering on the sidelines. Seth parked the car, looked at Renée and asked, "Are you ready for this?" Without waiting for her response, he got out of the car and shut the door.

As Seth started walking towards the playing field, a group of kids met him half way. Each of them eagerly attempted to get his attention. Some of them grabbed onto his arm, others patted him on the back. Still others rushed in front of his path almost causing him to trip.

Renée got out of the car and shut the door. She was going to catch up to Seth, but for a moment she hung back just watching. It was obvious that the kids absolutely adored him, and he in turn made them feel like there was something special about each one of them.

Stopping and realizing that Renée was not amongst the group of kids, he looked over his shoulder and called to her, "Come on, coach! We've some practicing to do!"

Renée smiled as she jogged to catch up with Seth and his followers.

# Chapter IV

Renée had the time of her life coaching the kids with Seth. She was hard pressed to remember a recent activity that had made her feel more at happy and at ease. (*I need to get out and have more fun, to relax, to play like when I was young*, she thought as she watched Seth dribble the soccer ball through a group of amazed kids.) They ran after him laughing while trying to get the ball. When one finally did, Seth bent over from exhaustion. Placing his hands on his knees, he attempted to catch his breath. He looked up, smiled at Renée, and then hollered, "Hey! We're not done yet! You can't leave me alone with these little hooligans!"

"I'm tired!" Renée called back to him. "Way too much energy!"

Seth told the kids that that was it for the day, and they had about five minutes and it would be time to leave. His comment was met with all kinds of opposition.

"Can't we stay just a little longer?" one little boy pleadingly asked Seth.

"Yeah," another chimed in, "just a little longer? Come

on, Seth, please?"

Seth laughed, tousled the hair of the small blonde-haired boy standing closest to him, and explained, "Tommy, you ask the same thing every week, and what do I *always* tell you?"

The slight boy moved the soccer ball between his feet and finally looked up at Seth and stated, "You always say that although we all have fun, we need a break, but not to worry because we can all come back next Saturday."

"And," Seth questioned him, "have I ever let you down?"

By this time most of the kids were heading off the field, but Tommy remained behind. "It's just that . . . it's just that. . ." the little boy looked around to make sure none of the other kids were watching. He pulled Seth's shirt so Seth would lean down, and he was able to whisper in his ear. "It's just that you treat me better than anyone. Seth, I wish you were my dad." The tiny boy caught Seth in an enormous bear hug, abruptly let go, and left to catch up with the other kids who were already off the field.

Seth was dumbfounded for a moment. Then he turned to Renée and asked, "Did you hear that?"

"Every word," Renée said with a smile. "Every word."

When Seth and Renée got back from soccer practice, they were greeted by a very angry Mel who was sitting on the deck drinking coffee. He glared at them as they walked to the house from the driveway.

"Hi," Renée said. She knew from Mel's expression that he was beyond angry. Hoping he would not blow up in front of Seth, she quickly began to explain where she had been. "I went with Seth to soccer practice. I told you about it before we left. Do you remember me waking you up?"

"No," Mel said angrily staring straight ahead.

"Oh," Renée said uncomfortably shifting her weight form one leg to the other. "We really weren't gone for very long, and well, we're back now."

"No crap," Mel remarked sarcastically as he lit a cigarette.

Mel continued to stare straight ahead as an uncomfortable silence took over. "Well," Seth finally said breaking the tension, "I'm all sweaty, so I think I'm going to go in and shower. Thanks for coming with me, Renée. It really meant a lot to the kids." As he opened the door and was about to go inside, he turned and said to Mel, "Hey, Mel, maybe you'd like to come with us sometime. The kids would get a kick out of it, and I think you would too."

Renée looked up sadly at Seth. She knew what he was trying to do, and she appreciated it. However, she knew that Mel looked at Seth's participation with the kids as stupid and a waste of time. Besides, that would mean that he would actually have to get up before noon on a Saturday.

Mel laughed, gave Seth a *you've got to be kidding me* look, and said, "No thanks, Seth. I'll leave the running around after little kids to you and Renée. The two of you seem to enjoy it *far* more than I ever would."

Seth just shrugged his shoulders and went into the house.

Renée sat in the chair next to Mel. He seemed to have cooled down somewhat from when they had first arrived. Renée was relieved to see this, as she had grown so tired of fighting with him. With each fight the distance between them was growing larger and larger. It seemed the harder Renée tried, the more Mel would push her away. She thought she would give it one more attempt. "Mel, I saw an ad in the paper for hot air balloon rides. Would you like to go? It might be fun."

"What?" Mel remarked looking at Renée like she had asked the stupidest question he had ever heard. "Ah, yeah, Renée, you say we don't have money, and then you suggest we waste it on something dumb like that? Don't you ever use your head? Are you this stupid all the time or is it just around me?"

Renée hung her head and silently walked towards the door. When she reached out to grab the handle and open it, Mel pushed her to the side and stood in front of her blocking her way.

Regaining her balance by holding onto the railing of the steps, she was frightened by his actions. Startled and upset she asked, "What're you doing?"

"I'm not done talking with you, Renée, my fiancé," Mel said crossing his arms in front of him and staring angrily at her.

Renée looked at Mel wondering why he had to behave like this. "What's wrong?" Renée questioned reaching for Mel's arm.

He sharply pulled it away, like an upset child, and hissed, "Don't touch me. I can't believe that you'd be so stupid not to know what's bothering me. But why should that surprise me? Hmmmmmm let me think about this for a minute, Renée. You leave all morning to hang out with your *boyfriend*, and I'm supposed to be fine with this?" The angrier he got, the louder his voice became.

"Mel," Renée began, "What. . ."

Before she could finish her sentence, Mel pushed her against the railing. She grabbed onto it again, balancing herself, so she would not fall. Mel took another step toward her, brought his face within inches of hers, and continued. "Why do you have to whore around like this? My God, Renée, is it too much to ask that my fiancé doesn't go out on dates with other guys? What's the deal? You want him that badly? Is that it?"

"It's not like that, Mel. Seth and I are just friends. This morning I tried to wake you up to see if you wanted to come with us, but you told me to leave you alone." Renée started to cry. She raised her hand to wipe away the tears. (*Why was he treating her like this?*)

"Whatever," Mel said pushing past her. He walked

down the steps and threw his coffee cup at the side of the garage. It smashed into small pieces and fell to the ground. "I'm leaving, Renée, and I'm not sure when I'm gonna be back." He turned around and yelled at her, "I'm sick and tired of you whoring around!"

Before Renée could say anything, he got in his car and drove away.

Renée's mouth fell open as she sadly watched him leave. She stood still clinging to the railing, staring at the empty road. Finally, feeling her body relax, she slumped down on the steps. Holding her head in her hands, tears streamed down her cheeks. (*What am I going to do? Is there any way out?*) Mel had always been moody, but this was too much to take. She had had enough, but what could she do? To whom could she turn? Her family had made it quite clear where they stood on the issue: she had gotten herself into this mess, so she was the one who needed to get herself out. The reality of this idea did not help matters. In fact, it made it worse. She felt trapped, and she honestly did not know how she was going to get out of the predicament in which she was in.

Mel sped down the highway. After angrily driving for some time, he fumbled around the front seat, looking for his cell phone. He swerved, barely missing a car, as he found his way back into his lane.

Pressing number two on speed dial, a woman's voice came across the line. "Hello." Then she added seductively, "I was wondering when you'd call. I was getting a little lonely."

"I'm on my way," Mel huskily said in the phone. "After last night, I wasn't sure I would be able to walk . . ." He laughed and added in a low voice, "It's amazing what a good, uh, *backrub* will do for a person."

"Oooooo," she said getting excited, "you better hurry up and get here. I don't think I can wait much longer."

"Unlock your door 'cause I'm driving into your parking

lot. Give me three minutes, and I'll be up the stairs ready to go." He hung up his phone, parked his car, and ran towards the apartment building.

Renée sat quietly on the steps. She had dried her tears and stopped crying, but she was not yet ready to go into the house where she would inevitably, at some point, be confronted by Seth and Maggie. (*They both must think I'm the biggest fool*, Renée thought as she rubbed the back of her neck.) She felt a wave of embarrassment at recalling the events of the night before: Mel coming home drunk, picking a fight with Seth, and then hitting on Maggie. She wondered how long it would take before the two of them would get sick and tired of Mel's crap and move out. "Why would they put up with this if they didn't have to?" Renée questioned placing her head in her hands and rocking back and forth. (*And then what?* she wondered. But she did not want to think about it.) She was really enjoying having them around. In fact, there were times when she would find herself being glad that Mel was not at home, so she could spend time with Maggie and Seth. While neither of them had come right out and said it, they both seemed to be enjoying themselves, too.

"Isn't that something?" Renée asked quietly. "Two people I don't know all that well care more about me than my own fiancé." She half-heartedly laughed at this idea because if she hadn't, she would have begun to cry again.

"Hey, this spot taken?"

"Huh?" Renée turned around to see Seth standing over her smiling.

"Well?"

"Ah, no," Renée said slightly embarrassed. She moved over so Seth could sit down. "I didn't here you, sorry, I guess I was just lost in thought."

"I see," Seth said petting Tyon who was comfortably curled up in his arms.

Renée and Seth sat in silence for about five minutes when Seth finally suggested, "Renée, Maggie and I were talking about going on that hot air balloon ride. Maybe you'd have some fun if you came with us."

Renée sat staring at the pieces from the cup that Mel had thrown against the garage. (*I should probably pick those up before someone steps on them and gets their feet cut*, she thought absent-mindedly.)

"Well?" Seth inquired.

"Oh, I'm sorry, Seth . . . ah, yeah, I'd love to go, but I really don't have the money for it right now." Renée was surprised that Seth didn't mention anything about the fight she and Mel had just had. (*Maybe*, she thought hopefully, *he had been busy doing something else, and neither he nor Maggie had heard it*.) She stood up, walked towards the garage, and starting picking up the pieces from the cup.

Seth followed her, bent down to help, and simply stated, "Renée, I didn't ask you if you had the money, I asked you if you'd like to go with us. So, would you like to go or not?"

Renée tried to concentrate on picking up the pieces so she would not start crying. "Thank you," she said to Seth as he took the broken pieces from her hand and brought them to the garbage.

When he returned, Renée forced a smiled and asked, "What time are you guys planning on leaving?"

"As soon as we can get ready to go."

Renée crossed her arms in front of her. She looked down at some rocks and kicked them. "If you're sure it's okay," she said quietly, "then I'd like to go."

"Alright," Seth said half hugging her around the shoulders. "Have you ever been in a hot air balloon? I haven't, and I think it's going to be fun. You're not scared of heights, are you?"

"No," Renée said looking up into his dark eyes. "Are you?"

"Nope," Seth said and added conceitedly. "I'm not too scared of anything."

Renée started to laugh. "Oh, really? That's a pretty interesting comment."

"You don't believe me?" Seth asked trying to appear offended.

"Oh, sure, Seth. Whatever you say."

"Okay, okay, maybe I'm being a little cocky," he said with a smile. "But hey, let's get ready so we can get going."

Renée, Seth, and Maggie got into Seth's Camaro and headed to the fairgrounds where the balloon rides were being given. Maggie chatted nonstop about anything and everything on the way. Every once in a while, when Maggie would stop talking long enough to take a breath, Seth interjected a thought or an idea. Periodically, Renée would turn to Seth and smile or laugh at something Maggie had said, but for the most part, her mind was elsewhere as she stared out the window. (Why was he so mean to her? she wondered over and over. Was it something I've done? Could I've done something differently?) She looked from Seth to Maggie and was concerned with what they thought of her, particularly what they thought of her relationship with Mel. She wished it wasn't so complicated. (They must think I'm a complete idiot for staying with him. How couldn't they?)

"We're here!" Maggie's squeal of delight brought Renée back to the present moment. "Oh, this is going to be so much fun! Let's go!" Without waiting for Seth and Renée, she pushed Renée's seat forward and searched for the door handle. Finding it, she opened the door and bounded from the car.

"She's such a little kid," Renée laughed. "I really envy her enthusiasm."

As Renée was getting out of the car, Seth lightly grabbed her arm. "Hey, you doing okay?"

"Yeah, yeah, I'm fine," Renée said biting her bottom lip. But Seth was not convinced. "Hey, Renée, if you don't want to do this, you don't have to. I didn't mean to sound like I was pressuring you when I had asked you to come with us."

"Seth," Renée said trying to sound hurt, "you mean you drag me all the way out here, and now you're insinuating that you don't want me here? You're not getting out of *forcing* me to come with you guys that easily. Now, if you're thinking that this is going to be too expensive, well, I can understand that . . ." She held her chin high letting him know that she didn't want him to feel sorry for her.

"No," Seth laughed. "I just wanted to make sure you were up to this, and I guess you answered that question."

"Hey!" Seth and Renée heard Maggie yell. She was waiting in line waving her arms over her head. "You guys need to hurry up otherwise we're going to lose our turn! Come on!"

"We better get over there," Seth said, "otherwise we'll have to endure the wrath of Maggie!"

Fortunately, there were not as many people in line to go on the balloon ride as they had anticipated. Also, there were several balloons that were being launched at various times. One balloon would land, the people would get off, and another balloon would began rising into the sky. Renée saw a beautiful yellow and red striped balloon approaching the landing and hoped that would be the one on which the three of them would be riding.

"Tickets, tickets, please," an elderly man said as he held out his hand.

As Seth gave him his ticket, he asked, "Uh, have any of these crashed recently?"

"Oh, only about two or three of them," the man said with a twinkle is his eye.

"You're kidding, right?" Seth said with a nervous laugh.

The man shook his head and smiled. "Yes, yes, I was only teasing you. Have a nice ride, young man." He directed them to the balloon that Renée had hoped they would be riding.

"Here we go!" Maggie exclaimed poking her head between Seth and Renée as she stood behind them with one arm draped over each of their shoulders. "This is amazing! Don't you guys think?"

Renée had to admit the view was absolutely breathtaking. The higher the balloon rose, the more free she felt. She closed her eyes for a moment, and felt the light breeze blow across her face. All her worries, anxieties, and fears seemed to fall away from her. "This definitely was one of your better ideas," Renée remarked to Maggie as she opened her eyes. She glanced at Seth who was peering over the basket at the ground below. When the balloon initially had begun to ascend, he didn't look too sure of himself. However, now he looked relaxed and happy. Renée was very grateful that he had talked her into coming with them. The last thing she had wanted to do was sit at home alone and keep replaying over and over the events of earlier that day.

"Well, what do you think?" Seth asked turning his head towards Renée.

"Oh, Seth, this is absolutely amazing! Thank you, thank you so much for bringing me along and . . . well . . . just thank you."

"You bet," Seth replied. Renée was relieved he hadn't asked her *for what*?

# Chapter V

The next day, Sunday, the house was very still and quiet. Maggie, Renée, and Seth went to church while Mel slept in. This time, Renée did not even try to wake him. It bothered her that he had come home so late, again, but at least she was grateful that he had at least made it home. Renée had tucked the blankets up around his chin, kissed him on the cheek, and quietly left the house. It did not take too much persuading for Seth and Maggie to join her at the morning service. Normally, she would go herself, as Mel would never come with her. He had told her over and over that church was a waste of his time. He believed that if God wanted to find him, He knew where to look.

"Hmmmm," Seth said heading to the car after he, Maggie, and Renée walked out of the doors after the service was over, "that preacher really had a good message today. Didn't you guys think?" Renée did not say anything, as she was fiddling with the straps on her purse, so Seth continued, "I liked how he talked about how important it's to be true to yourself, believing in yourself, and putting your trust in God. Didn't you guys?"

Renée smiled and recited the verse she knew so well from *Luke 11:9-10*, "And so I tell you, keep on asking, and you will receive what you ask for. Keep on seeking, and you will find. Keep on knocking, and the door will be opened to you. For everyone who asks, receives. Everyone who seeks, finds. And to everyone who knocks, the door will be opened."

Seth stopped and stared at Renée admiringly. "Huh, I guess you were listening during the service. That's pretty impressive that you've that passage memorized."

Renée, embarrassed by Seth's praise, went on to explain, "I always liked that verse. When I was a little girl, I went to church a lot with my grandma. At that church was the most beautiful stained glass window with a picture of Jesus knocking at a door. The more carefully I looked at the picture, the more I realized that the door could only be opened from the outside, not the inside. Grandma was the one who explained to me why."

"Which is?" Seth imploringly asked.

"Well, see, Jesus will never force Himself on you. A person has to honestly seek Him, and then open their heart, or door, to Him. Eventually, even when things get tough, if a person has enough faith, Jesus will be there to see them through it."

Seth nodded in agreement. He knew at that moment that, Renée, maybe without even realizing it, had taken the first step in freeing herself of the unhealthy relationship in which she was in.

Maggie, oblivious to the conversation that Seth and Renée were having, commented, "I don't know." She leaned down to undo the strap on her sandal so she could take them off and walk barefoot. "To tell you the truth, I was more interested in the layout of the church. I was just thinking that if Joe and I'd ever get married, this might be the kind of place I'd like to tie the knot."

"Oh, really?" Renée questioned as she and Seth looked at her in surprise.

"Ah, Maggie," Seth asked obviously confused, "did I miss something in the past month or so?"

"What do you mean?" Maggie wondered.

"Well," Renée stated as if she and Seth were thinking the same thing, "not to point out the obvious, but this *is* the first time you've really said anything about getting married."

"Oh, really?" Maggie tried to sound as aloof as possible, but she was not succeeding as a grin spread across her face. She beamed as she smiled from ear to ear.

"Maggie May," Renée questioned as she stopped just before they were all going to pile into the car, "is there something you're not telling us?"

Maggie shrugged her shoulders as she opened the door and got in the back seat. Seth and Renée exchanged glances and also got into the car.

"So," Seth finally broke the silence, "come on, Maggie, the suspense is killing Renée!"

"Oh, please, like it's not you!" Renée laughed as she leaned over and playfully punched Seth in the shoulder.

Renée and Seth both turned around and looked at Maggie who was sitting in the back seat, arms smugly crossed over her chest. "Okay, okay," she finally said. "Yeah, we've been talking about it."

"And how much have you been, ah, talking about it?" Renée asked raising an eyebrow.

"Apparently long enough for Maggie to start checking out churches," Seth said with a smile.

"Now I know why I didn't have to plead with you too much to get you to come to church with us this morning," Renée said trying to sound offended. "You had an ulterior motive. You ought to be ashamed of yourself!"

"Really," Maggie said trying to sound annoyed, "the two of you are impossible." The three of them started to laugh.

"Honestly," Maggie continued in all sincerity, "I really love him. He is truly the most wonderful man I've ever dated. Believe you me, it shocked me more than anyone that I'm seriously considering settling down. He's kind, considerate, caring, smart, and he has a great sense of humor."

"And," Renée butted in, "it probably helps that he's pretty darn good looking!"

Maggie smiled and nodded in agreement.

"Oh, my gosh," Seth said trying to sound hurt and offended. "I can't believe that you two can be so shallow and superficial about looks."

Renée knew he was toying with them, but she playfully took the bait anyway. "Oh, so, Seth, you mean to tell us that you're one of those guys who doesn't care about looks? Hmmm," she turned towards Maggie, "looks like we've a rare gem of a guy here . . ."

"Or a real big liar!" Maggie interrupted laughing from the back seat. Renée and Maggie both continued looking at Seth trying to contain their laughter. "Well, no comment, Seth?"

"Okay, okay, yes," Seth admitted. "Looks do matter. Now before the two of you call *me* shallow, come on, let me finish."

Maggie and Renée were intently waiting for Seth to continue. "Well?" Renée finally asked.

"Okay," Seth explained, "a lot of people say that looks don't matter, but I disagree. When you meet someone what's the first thing you notice? It's probably not that they've a great sense of humor, or that they're really intelligent, or that they're kind and generous. No, the first thing is their looks. But that doesn't mean that someone who you think is super hot will, after you've gotten to know them better, become less attractive because of their personality. The opposite is also true. Someone who I might think might be okay looking, might, after I've gotten to know her better, become really good looking to me. Also, there has to be chemistry between two people for it to work. You guys both know what I mean. Call me superficial if you want, but it's true. Both of you know it whether you want to admit it or not."

"Okay, okay, Seth," Maggie said suppressing a yawn. "Renée and I are both convinced that you're not as superficial as we thought. We both get it, right Renée?"

Renée silently nodded as she reminisced over what Seth had just explained. (*He's a very wise man*, she concluded. *A very wise man who's become even better looking.*)

When Renée, Maggie, and Seth opened the door after arriving home from church, they were greeted with the wonderful aroma of a homemade breakfast of bacon, eggs, and pancakes. Mel was up and in the process of cooking. He was clad in only a pair of boxers, and over that he had a faded apron that read *Kiss the Cook*. Seth looked at him standing barefoot in the kitchen. Even in spite of his shaved head, Seth had to admit that Mel was a good looking man. (*Maybe that's what Renée sees in him.*)

"Hey, hey," Mel said turning to greet them while flipping a pancake. Thought you sinners might be hungry when you got home." Renée, Maggie, and Seth looked at each other dumbfounded. (*What's with the sudden change?* They all seemed to silently ask.) Mel, seeming to hear what they were not saying, set down his spatula and walked over to Renée. Putting his arms around her, he began apologetically, "Honey, I'm so sorry I haven't been in the greatest of moods lately, and I'm sorry that I've been taking it out on you." He looked deeply into her brown eyes. "Can you find it in your heart to forgive me for being such a fool? I truly am so, so very sorry."

Renée felt Mel's arms around her, and her first instinct was to push him away. Although he appeared to be honestly asking for her forgiveness, a part of her questioned his sincerity. (*What does he want?* she wondered as he held her tightly. *The only time he treats me this well is when he needs something.*)

Seth and Maggie gave each other a puzzled look and began to walk out of the kitchen when Mel called, "Hey, where do the two of you think you're going? I didn't make this much food just for the two of us you know. Also," he added with repentance in his voice, "I haven't been the best to the two of you either, and I'm truly very sorry." He looked up earnestly at Seth and Maggie.

"Okay," commented Maggie cautiously. "I'm hungry; you didn't poison the food, did you?" she asked smiling but with a hint of seriousness in her voice.

Mel started to laugh. "No, Maggie! Do you think I'd honestly do something like that?"

Seth was not so sure. He was a pretty good study of people, and there was something about Mel's behavior that just was not adding up. He did not like him. More importantly, he did not trust him. It was going to take more than just a home cooked breakfast for him to change his mind, and he sensed that Mel knew that by the way he was looking at him. "I'm really not that hungry, but thanks anyway, Mel. I've a few errands to run." He turned to Renée, "I'll be back in about an hour or so. What'd you guys have planned for this afternoon?"

Renée shook her shoulders. "I don't know. It's supposed to be nice out today, maybe all of us could go to the lake or something. . ."

"Yeah," Mel interrupted, "when you get back, Seth, why don't we all go out to my dad's? We can use his boat and go waterskiing." He gave Seth a superior smile as he kissed Renée on the cheek. "Would that make you happy, baby? I'd like to see you in a bikini."

Renée turned red as she turned away from Mel and started to dish up some eggs. Then she hesitantly responded, "That does sound like a lot of fun. Don't you guys think?"

"Uh, huh," Maggie said between bites from the pancakes stacked on her plate. "Yeah, I'm game. You know Mel, I was kind of skeptical of your cooking, but these pancakes are really, really good. Thanks for making breakfast."

"No problem, Mags. Help yourself to as much as you want. With Seth not eating, there's bound to be a lot of extra," he said as he cockily glanced at Seth.

"I'll be back in about an hour," Seth said over his shoulder as he headed out the door. "Skiing sounds like a good time, count me in."

As Seth was driving to get a burger from a fast food place, thoughts of Mel and the way he treated Renée kept filling his mind. There was no doubt about it- Mel totally repulsed him. It was becoming more and more difficult for him to see him and Renée together. (*And what was with the "lovey-dovey" act this morning*? he wondered as he spoke into the speaker at the drive-thru.) Maybe it was juvenile, but he was not about to eat anything that Mel had prepared. Not that he was afraid that Mel would try to poison him; it was just that God only knows where his hands had been, and he sure as hell did not want him touching anything he was going to put into his mouth. He knew Mel was up to something, and he had a sneaking suspicion that Renée was thinking the same thing. "He's definitely a master manipulator," Seth said aloud as he took a bite of his burger. "But Renée's a big girl." Acknowledging this did not stop the unease rising from the pit of his stomach.

Seth knew the real reason he had had to leave without breakfast had nothing to do with Mel's cooking. As difficult as it was for him to admit, he was falling in love with Renée. And there was nothing he or his heart was able to do about it.

The drive to Mel's dad's place was a pretty one. The wild flowers along the road were in full bloom and delicately spread out on the side of the road looking like someone had randomly planted them there. The trees, lush and green, waved in the slight breeze as the sun guided them in a westward direction down the highway. He lived on a private lake in a very wealthy neighborhood. Renée leaned back in the seat and tried to get comfortable. She turned her head and smiled as she looked at Seth and Maggie. She was so grateful that all of them were going skiing that afternoon. The tension between Seth and Mel had been escalating, and she hoped that a fun day in the sun might put a damper on it. Mel's behavior that morning had been a welcomed changed. However, there was a hint of suspicion that loomed within Renée's mind, particularly after the way he had looked at Seth. (*Was she being over protective? Wasn't she just looking out for the best interest of a good friend of hers?*) Although she was not proud of it, she knew the answer was no. Unintentionally, she had allowed Seth to become closer to her than just a friend. With each day, it was getting more and more complicated . . . She loved Mel, but there were many times when she wondered if she was truly in love with him. She thought again of what Maggie had said about being in love or in love with the *idea* of being in love. She cared deeply about Seth, but the feelings that she felt towards him- she did not know exactly what to make of them. He was, truly, one of the best friends she had ever had. He always seemed to know just what to say and just when she needed to hear it. She wondered if he was also feeling confused about his relationship with her.

". . . that's a good idea, don't you think?" Mel said glancing at her.

"What?" Renée asked as she straightened up in her seat. "I'm sorry, Mel, what did you say?"

Mel looked out the window, rolled his eyes, and turned back to Renée. "Have you been listening to anything I've been saying?" He glared at her. "Apparently not," he said between clenched teeth as he gripped the steering wheel more tightly.

After a moment of silence, Mel completely changed his mannerism. He turned to Renée and sweetly said, "Sorry I lost my cool, honey. It's just that we don't get to talk as much as we used to. When we do have a chance, it seems like you don't care to hear what's on my mind."

"Sorry, Mel, what was it that you were saying?"

Mel sighed heavily. "Well," he finally began, "I know we don't have a lot of money, and it's probably unfair of me to ask this, but I really, really want to get a new car."

"Huh?" Renée asked confusedly. "Is there something wrong with this one?"

"Honey, are you serious? Do you really not know?" Mel asked in disbelief as he glanced at Renée.

She shook her head no.

"Of course you wouldn't," he continued condescendingly. "You only know about those old *antiquey* cars you look at in the car magazine or a beater like the one Seth drives."

Renée glanced over her shoulder. "You're so fortunate that Seth's sleeping. If he ever heard you talking about his car like that, he'd probably knock you into next week." Renée shook her head in obvious disagreement. "His car is anything but an old beater. I don't think you realize how much that car is worth."

"Okay, okay." Mel continued in his manipulative way of speaking, "I don't want to get in a fight with you, baby, it's just that my car is *not* in the greatest condition, and I really need to get a new one. I was almost worried about driving it out to my dad's today. I was afraid it would break down on the side of the road."

Renée looked around the interior of the vehicle. She knew that she could not tell much without looking under the hood, but if the mess on the inside was any indication of how Mel cared for his vehicle, then maybe he was right. Maybe his car was turning into a pile of junk because he was too lazy to take it in and get it serviced regularly. However, she was having a difficult time believing the car was in as bad shape as Mel was trying to make it out to be. "So, why don't you take out a loan to buy a new vehicle?" Renée finally asked.

Renée could tell from the look on Mel's face and the tightening of his jaw that he was getting extremely annoyed with her lack of cooperation in securing a new vehicle for him as soon as possible. "Uh, I did, but unfortunately, I didn't qualify. I've some things on my credit report that aren't my fault- bills that they *said* I didn't pay, but I know I did."

"Well," Renée sincerely proposed, "maybe you should get a copy of your credit report, fix it, and then you could reapply for a loan."

"But that could take a long time," Mel whined annoyingly. "I've another idea . . ."

"Yes."

"Well, if you co-signed for a vehicle, then I could get one earlier than if I had to go through the hassle of trying to fix my credit score and then wait to get a vehicle."

"Uh, I don't know if I feel comfortable doing that. I mean, we're really strapped financially the way it is, and if we add a car payment each month. . ." She looked doubtful. "Mel, it's difficult for us to make ends meet the way it is. I just don't think we could afford it."

"Whatever," Mel sneered staring straight ahead. "If it was something *you* wanted, then you'd find a way to afford it. There you go being selfish again."

"What?" Renée asked with hurt and disappointment in her voice. "How can you even say that? You know I work as hard as I can to make ends meet. Do you think I like it that we live from pay check to pay check? Don't you think I'd like to have some extra money to go out and do things?"

"Didn't seem to stop you the other day when you went on that stupid balloon ride."

Renée felt her face redden. She contemplated for a while whether to tell him the truth about who had bought the ticket. Realizing it was probably the honest thing to do, she stated as calmly as possible, "Mel, Seth paid for my ticket that day. He felt sorry for me because you stormed out of the house after you threw your coffee cup against the garage. Or don't you remember?"

"Oh, sure," Mel haughtily commented, "blame it all on me. God, Renée, do you ever take any responsibility for your actions? Why can't you just admit that you're too selfish to let me get a car?"

"You're thinking about getting a new car?" Seth's voice questioned from the back seat. "What's wrong with this car, Mel?"

Mel nervously glanced in the rearview mirror at Seth. "Hey, man," he casually said, "thought you and Maggie were sleeping back there, the two of you've been so quiet."

"We were," Maggie annoyingly commented, "until all the fighting woke us up. Honestly, what're the two of you arguing about this time?"

"Hey," Mel laughed as he glanced out the corner of his eye at Renée who was sitting angrily with her arms crossed over her chest. "We weren't really arguing. Were we baby? We were just discussing the possibility of us getting a different vehicle. No big deal."

As they pulled into the long driveway leading to Mel's dad's house, Maggie asked, "Why don't you just ask your dad for the money for a new vehicle? Looks like he has enough of it."

"Maybe I will," Mel said as he stopped the car and put it into park. "Maybe I will."

Renée took a deep breath and shook her head from side to side. Mel knew how she felt about always asking his dad for help with financial matters. It bothered her that every time Mel wanted something, instead of working out a way to pay for it, he would go to his dad. It upset her, especially when she would specifically remind Mel that the two of them could not afford it, and he would go behind her back anyway. It was upsetting, as the two of them were supposed to be trying to build a life together. She did not want to exclude his dad from their lives, but she believed that some boundaries needed to be established. Renée was about to say something, then she decided better of it. She had learned the hard way that Mel could be sweet, loving, charming, and debonair when they were around other people. But behind closed doors, he could turn into a mean, cold-hearted, cruel man. And it was especially worse if Renée had said or done something to upset him in front of anyone.

"Wow!" Maggie exclaimed shutting the car door. "This place's just gorgeous! What *does* your dad do for a living?"

"Yeah, it's good enough, I guess. He's only a surgeon, so this is about all he can afford."

Mel led the way to the front door. As he reached to open it, he found it locked. "What the hell?" he mumbled in blatant annoyance. There was a note taped to the door. Mel grabbed it and read aloud, "Mel and friends, sorry I won't be around this afternoon. I was called in on an emergency. Go ahead and use the boat, you know where the key is. Be careful, have fun, and please put everything back where you take it from. Love, Dad." Mel crumbled the note and tossed it onto the front lawn.

"So what do we do now?" Maggie questioned.

"Well, duh," Mel said belittlingly, "I *do* have a key for the guesthouse."

Seth looked around him at his surroundings. Although Seth had known Mel when they were younger, he had never been out to his dad's place. He did not know much about Mel's childhood except that his parents had gotten divorced when he was just a kid. Because of all the trouble Mel had gotten into in his youth, neither parent really wanted him around. He would stay with one parent for awhile until he outwore his welcome, and then he would live with the other until the same thing would happen. Seth tried to remember the first time he had met Mel, and he was pretty certain it was when they were in their early teens. One thing that Seth did know about Mel was that his dad had money, and lots of it. The large, lakeside home must have cost a fortune, not to mention all the landscaping and perfectly manicured flower gardens decorating the property. Seth looked at Renée. (*So maybe this is also why Renée is so attracted to Mel*). He scratched his head with perplexity. It struck him as odd that Renée would be the kind of woman who would be so easily swayed by money. It just did not add up. He finally concluded that maybe he did not know her as well as he thought he did.

"It sucks that my dad's not home. Now we can't get in the house. Apparently he locked us out because he doesn't trust me. What a loser," Mel snorted. "But at least he said we could take the boat out. If you girls need to change, go use the guest house. Seth, if you're ready, get off your lazy ass and help me get the boat in the lake, at least I know where the key is for that."

"Yeah, yeah, sure," Seth said.

"Well, Maggie and I are going to go to the guest house then. Should we meet you guys down at the water?" Renée looked from Seth to Mel. Mel dug in his pocket, and not bothering to acknowledge that Renée had asked him a question, rudely tossed her the key.

Seth, irritated at how disrespectful Mel was being, looked at her and said, "See you ladies there. You two better not be lollygagging either. The water's perfect for skiing so hurry up!" He gave Renée a good natured smile and pointed towards the guest house. He watched as the sun shone through the trees onto her face. Again, he was struck by how truly beautiful she was.

"Oh, man, I never thought I was gonna get a break from

her," Mel said to Seth as he opened the small cooler he was carrying, took out a beer, and slammed it. After he squeezed the can and then threw it in the trees, he reached for another and asked Seth, "You want one?"

"No," Seth said. "No, I'm good thanks." Then he cautiously added, "Hey, Mel, aren't you going to be driving the boat?"

"Yeah, so?" Mel looked at Seth with utter confusion he guzzled the beer he had just opened. Tossing the empty can carelessly into of one of the perfectly manicured flower gardens, he rummaged through the cooler and grabbed another.

"Well, not to point out the obvious, but don't you think you might want to slow down especially when you're going to be in the driver's seat?"

"What the hell, Seth, when did you turn into such a pansy? God, you're worse than Renée harping on me about my drinking. I'm just having a few beers! It's not like I'm gonna to get drunk or anything. I thought we came out here to have some fun."

"Yeah," Seth said holding his ground, "but I don't think it's going to be too much fun if we end up smashing up your dad's boat or if someone gets hurt. Are you forgetting you're going to be pulling a skier behind you?"

"You know what, if you don't want to come along, fine. Sit on the damned deck if it makes you happy." Mel took off angrily towards the boat landing and started lowering the boat into the water.

Seth followed. Although inside he was seething, he was not going to give Mel the satisfaction of knowing it. Also, it would be a cold day in hell when he would leave him alone with Maggie and Renée in the boat the way he was tossing back beers. He calmed himself and said, "Okay, okay. Take it easy, Mel. You're right. We're all here to have a good time, so let's do it."

Before Mel had a chance to comment, Renée and

Maggie began walking to the edge of the dock, and then they both got into the boat.

"Who's going to go first?" Mel questioned as he lit a cigarette. "Maggie?" She was wearing a fuchsia bikini, and Mel had been eyeing her.

"Uh, no," Maggie said taking a seat next to Seth towards the back. "I'm not too interested in skiing." She looked at Renée and offered, "Renée, I bet you're a good skier considering how athletic you are, how about you go?"

"Oh, yeah, she's really good," Mel said rolling his eyes. "I guess I'll have to show everyone how it's done. Seth, you know how to drive, right?" Seth nodded. "Okay, good." Mel tossed the butt of his cigarette into the water, fastened his lifejacket, and then dove off the front of the boat.

"Do you think he's sober enough to ski?" Maggie worriedly whispered following Seth as he got into the driver's seat.

"If not, maybe the son-of-a-bitch will drown," Seth said only loud enough for Maggie to hear. She covered her mouth in an attempt to suppress a giggle.

As Mel surfaced and began placing his feet in the skis that Renée had set in the water, he hollered, "Damn! The water is cold!"

"Oh, suck it up!" Seth called from the driver's seat. "Are you ready to ski or what?"

"Yeah, yeah, just let me get these skis fastened, and I'll show all of you how it's done."

"Sure you will," Maggie said under her breath. "Show everyone how you can take a nose dive into the water. You bet."

Renée started laughing. "He's really a good skier, Maggie. I think you'll be impressed."

"Okay!" Mel hollered as he held the handle attached to the rope tightly between his bent knees. His skis were facing up, ready to ride on top of the water. "Hit it!"

Seth moved the accelerator forward, and the boat rapidly began to pick up speed. Renée looked back as she watched Mel pop out of the water and gracefully ride on top of the waves. She smiled. (*He's good, really good.*) He stayed in the wake, making sure of his balance and checking his footing. Then, he dropped one ski.

Seth glanced over his shoulder. "I didn't know he was going to slalom! I wish he would've told us. Is anyone in the way of his ski?"

"No, all's clear," Maggie said bringing her hand up to shield her eyes from the sun. "I'm impressed. He's a lot better than I thought he'd be." Mel continued to go in and out of the wake area, bending closer and closer to the water, until he reached down and touched it with his hand.

"Oh, he's down. Stop the boat!" Renée called out to Seth. "Let's pick up Mel, and then go and get the other ski."

Seth turned around the boat and headed in Mel's direction. (*He's quite the talented ski*er, Seth thought as he turned the wheel and slowed down so Mel could climb aboard. *It's probably all the summer days he got to spend on the lake.*) Seth thought about his own childhood. His parents never had a lot of money. During the summer, ever since he could remember, he had had a job. He had worked long hours, so he could afford new clothes when school would start in the fall. When he had gotten older, any extra money that he had went towards the restoration of Princess. (*What a different world I grew up in than that of Mel's,* Seth thought as he glanced at Mel who was drying off with the beach towel Renée had handed him.)Mel was grinning from ear to ear as he took a drink from the beer he had just opened.

"So," Mel said sitting down, "who's going to follow that? Damn, I'm good. Wouldn't you admit, Seth? Think you can match any of the stuff I did out there?"

"Probably not," Seth answered honestly. "But maybe

Renée can."

Mel looked at Renée and started laughing. "Yeah, right! I highly doubt that, especially when I taught her everything she knows about skiing. Right, Renée?"

"Uh, I don't know. I guess," she quietly commented as she zipped her lifejacket. Then she carefully asked Mel, "Say, while you're finishing up your beer, do you think Seth could drive?"

"Uh, no," Mel scoffed at the suggestion. "No, I'm driving. I can easily drive without spilling a drop. But thanks for being so concerned about me, worried that I'm going to spill my beer," he added rolling his eyes. "Why don't you get in the water? We'll go get the other ski, because I know you can't get up on one, and then we'll be back to get you."

"Uh," Renée stammered looking uncertain, "are you sure you're okay to drive considering the amount you've had to drink?"

"Whatever! God, Renée, what do you think I've been sucking on a hose from a mysterious keg in the water while I was skiing? Give me a break. Do you want to ski or what?"

Renée looked at Mel. "Yes, I want to ski, but just please be careful. Don't go too fast, okay?"

"Yeah, yeah, just get in the water and we'll come around to pick you up." Renée jumped in the water and waited for the boat to get back so she could put on the other ski.

"Ready?" Mel yelled from the driver's seat?

Renée raised her hand, thumb in the air, and screamed, "Hit it!" Just like that, she was up on top of the water.

Seth had to hand it to her; he was really impressed. Whether it was true about Mel teaching her everything he knew or not, he had to admit that Renée could ski. She gracefully glided through the water. "Wow, look at her!" Seth commented to no one in particular.

"Whew! Go Renée!" Maggie called from the back of

the boat. Then she turned towards Mel and said, "Looks like you've some competition, and I thought you said she wasn't any good."

"She's not that good," Mel said as he moved the lever to speed up the boat. "Let's see how she does with a little more speed."

"Must not be bothering her at all," Seth said laughing, "because she just dropped a ski. Way to go, Renée!" She took one hand off the rope and with a huge smile of accomplishment on her face, she waved.

"What the hell's she trying to prove?" Mel mumbled under his breath. "Let's see how well she does with this." Without warning, he drove the boat so close to the dock that Renée almost hit it. Startled, she abruptly let go of the rope and tumbled through the water. Seth and Maggie ducked just in time as the ski rope whipped past their heads.

Seth turned around to see Renée floating lifelessly in the water. "Oh, my God, I think she's hurt!" He turned to Mel and angrily yelled, "Turn the boat around, hurry up, man!"

"Yeah, yeah, all that's probably hurt is her pride because she bit it," he arrogantly assumed as he turned the steering wheel.

As they came closer to Renée, Seth could see the fear in her eyes as she grimaced with pain. Held up by her lifejacket, she floated up and down with the waves as she cradled her left arm closely to her chest. Without hesitation, Seth dove into the water. As he swam closer, he could see tears streaming down her face. "Renée," he questioned gently as he treaded water beside her, "are you okay?"

Unable to catch her breath, Renée shook her head from side to side. She was still clutching her arm tightly to her lifejacket. "Is it your arm? Did you hurt your arm?" Renée nodded. "Okay, hold still, I'm going to bring you over to the boat." Seth carefully grabbed the back of her lifejacket and gently guided her through the water. "You're going to be okay. I'm going to lift you into the boat." He angrily yelled at Mel who was finishing the last of beer and smoking a cigarette, "How about a little bit of help, buddy? I think your fiancé just broke her arm!"

"Oh, my God, Renée," Mel asked with mock sincerity as he dropped his beer can and flicked his cigarette butt into the water. "Are you okay, honey? Let me help you." Seth turned her towards the back of the boat by the ladder. Mel grabbed her by the armpits and lifted her out of the water. "Careful, man!" Seth barked. "She's hurt, okay?"

Mel sneered, "Yeah, yeah. I heard you."

As Seth climbed in after her, the only thing he had on his mind was that this was no accident. "We need to get her to the emergency room, now!" Seth hollered at Mel.

"What? Are you a doctor?" Mel asked him sharply. He turned to Renée, "Are you okay? Do you need to go to the hospital?"

Renée finally found her voice and weakly replied still holding her arm, "It hurts. I can't move it."

"Okay, okay," Mel explained. "I didn't think it was *that* bad." Assuming his spot in the driver's seat, he pushed the accelerator forward and sulkily added, "Guess this ends our day at the lake."

Seth drove to the hospital. Fortunately, it had not taken too much convincing on his part to get Mel, who had too much to drink, to let him drive. Mel could see in Seth's eyes that if he had put up any resistance, Seth would probably have hit him. The only demand Mel had made in order to allow Seth to drive his car was that he got to listen to *his* music. Mel had also insisted that since he wasn't driving, he had to sit in the back with Renée to make sure she was okay. (*Kind of late for faking that you care now*, Seth thought.)

Seth kept playing over and over in his head what had

happened. He was certain that Mel had done it on purpose. He looked out the window watching the trees fly by. In spite of Mel's music being so loud, Seth could hear Mel laugh as he animatedly talked on his cell phone. Finally, he turned to Maggie, who was sitting in the front seat with him, and whispered, "I think he did it on purpose."

Maggie looked directly into Seth's eyes, anger filling her own, and nodded. "I was thinking the same thing. Stupid son-of-a-bitch, I wish someone would knock him on his ass. Say, Seth," she said with an evil grin, "know of anyone who could beat the crap out of him? I'm willing to pay. . ."

Seth, although he tried not to, started laughing.

Mel, who had finally ended his cell phone conversation, suspiciously questioned staring over the seat at Seth and Maggie, "What's going on up there?"

"Nothing," Maggie said with defiance. "Do you think we can turn this crap music down, so we can hear ourselves think? If not, we might get into an *accident*." She shot a look at Mel that even startled Seth. She did not like Mel, and at that point she did not seem too worried about letting him know how she really felt.

"Whatever," Mel commented as he reached over the seat to change the CD. In doing so, he bumped Seth's elbow causing him to swerve in the other lane, nearly hitting a car.

"Sit your ass down!" Seth yelled glaring at Mel.

"Like it's *my* fault you don't know how to drive!" Mel yelled as he sat back down. When he did, he knocked into Renée causing her arm to hit against the side of the door. She let out a low moan from the pain as tears began to stream down her face.

Finally arriving at the hospital, Seth stopped in front of the Emergency Room door.

"You guys go in," Mel said. "I hate hospitals with a passion, so I'll go park the car."

"What?" Seth asked in disbelief. "You're not going to go in with her?"

"No, no, man. Just take her in. Renée knows I can't stand hospitals." Mel looked from side to side like he was watching for someone.

Seth couldn't believe Mel would not go with her, but he did not have time to give it much thought. He was too worried about Renée. "Okay, but don't drive any further than to that parking spot. We don't need you getting a DUI." Seth pointed to a spot and then turned to Maggie. "Maggie, let's get her inside."

After seeing the doctor and having x-rays, Renée was elated to find that her arm was not broken but rather severely sprained. The three things the doctor prescribed for her were a pain reliever, ice, and time. He explained to Renée that it would hurt for about a week, and then she would be back to normal.

Walking with Seth and Maggie out the doors of the Emergency Room, Renée was hurt and upset that Mel had not been there with her. Seeing his parked car, she looked for him. He was not inside it. Then she saw him sauntering across the parking lot towards them.

"Well," Seth stated as Mel came closer, "Renée's going to be okay." (*As if you care,* he wanted to say.)

"Alright, great honey, I was so worried," Mel said giving Renée a hug.

Seth glared at him. (*You stupid son-of-a-bitch. Why the hell couldn't you have gone in with her? Scared of hospitals, my ass.*) Then he wondered, asking, "Where were you?"

"Not to point out the obvious," Mel spat back, "but some of us do have jobs. . ."

Before Mel could continue, Maggie asked, butting in sarcastically, "Not to point out the obvious, but what the hell does that have to do with anything? "

It was Mel's turn to interrupt. "Hey, I'm not the one

who was getting all in my face about where I was. It's Seth fault."

"Little defensive, aren't you?" Seth asked. "I was just wondering where you had been."

"Whatever," Mel mumbled under his breath. "Do you think I like working on a Sunday? Huh?" He glared at Seth and then at Maggie. "When someone needs me, it's my business to be there."

Maggie and Seth exchanged puzzled looks. (*Why does he keep referring to his work?* they both seemed to question.)

"Mel," Seth asked with suspicion, "what *exactly* is your business, again?"

"Why don't the two of you just relax?" Mel questioned as he nervously rocked from side to side. "Shouldn't we be concentrating on Renée? If the two of you are *really* that interested in what I do for a living, which may be a bit too complicated for you to understand, I'll gladly take you through it step by step when we get home. As for now, all the two of you really need to be concerned with is how Renée's doing."

Seth was extremely concerned about Renée. That was probably why the sickening feeling he had in his stomach would not go away. (*Could Mel be selling drugs? Is that his business? Would he really be that stupid?*)

# Chapter VI

In the evening, just when the sun was setting, Seth and Renée usually found themselves sitting on *The Stoop*. They would go over and discuss the events of the day. Renée had come to really enjoy this time with Seth, and he also enjoyed spending time with her. The two of them entertained themselves by talking about all kinds of different topics from world peace to baseball. However, one subject Seth never brought up was the idea that Mel might be selling drugs. Seth had thought about it over and over, but he just did not know what to do. Without any proof, it was difficult to prove. If he falsely accused, Mel, he might loose Renée's confidence forever. He had thought about talking with Maggie about it- as the two of them often talked, and they both wondered what the hell Renée was doing with Mel- but Seth knew Mel did not like Maggie. He worried that if he and Maggie falsely accused him, it would just make matters worse. (*No*, Seth finally decided, *if my inclination is correct and he's selling, it'll only be a matter of time before he gets caught. Hopefully before that time, Renée will have made the decision to leave him.*)

Seth silently observed how Mel mistreated Renée, and he could not understand why she stayed with him. There were many times he got the feeling that Renée wondered the same thing. But Renée never brought up the topic of her relationship with Mel, and Seth tried to remind himself that it truly was not any of his business.

That evening, Renée looked particularly perplexed when she and Seth sat in their usual spots. "What's up?" Seth finally asked looking at Renée.

"Long day at work," she sighed as she stretched out her legs. "There's this little boy who absolutely won't trust anyone. It's really sad. He feels like all adults are out to get him."

"Any particular reason?"

"Yeah, there's a good reason." Before she got to the reason, she thought it was important to give Seth some background information about the boy. "This little boy has been part of one of the after school programs for as long as he has been old enough to join. So I've known him for a few years already. Anyway, he used to be so trusting, but that all changed when one of his teachers at school accused him of cheating."

"Huh?" Seth sounded surprised.

"Well, there's more to it than that. See, his family doesn't have a lot of money. His parents are both very hard workers, but neither of them went to college. Well, you know that an education can open the doors to better jobs- not always, of course- but most of the time. His parents are the most honest, trustworthy people I know, and their son would never get away with that kind of behavior."

"So," Seth interjected, "the teacher told the parents that the little boy had been cheating, the parents sided with the teacher, and the little boy was crushed because he really hadn't been cheating."

"Exactly," Renée confirmed.

"Hmmm, how old is he?"

"He's ten, and he's in fifth grade."

"Ouch, that's tough for a kid's ego, especially for a boy at that age. You know? They're at that age when they're trying to fit in and be cool. Yet they still want the approval of their teachers. Was the teacher justified in accusing him?"

"No," Renée said matter-of-fact. "No, she wasn't."

"And you know this how?"

"Like I said, I've known this boy for some time now, about three, almost four years. When I noticed his behavior was different, I asked him what was going on. At first, he was defiant and said, 'You wouldn't care anyway.' Finally, he told me what had happened. I know his teacher because her kids used to come to the after school program. I really felt sorry for them because she's a real "b" word."

Seth started laughing. "Jeez, Renée, I don't think I've ever heard you use such vulgarities."

Renée smiled, rolled her eyes, and continued. "Anyway, you know the type. She thinks she knows everything, and what she doesn't know, she makes up so people won't know that she doesn't know everything. Her kids only attended our program for one school year. She decided they didn't belong with people of a, how did she put it? - oh, I remember- lesser socio-economic status."

"Hmmm, I didn't know teachers made six figures now a day."

"No kidding. She's just the type of person that thinks she's a lot better than she is. She looks down her nose at others, particularly people that don't have a college education."

"Ah, and neither of this boy's parents do, do they?"

"No, they don't. The kids had to write a summary of a book they had read, and she had accused him of copying it. She had told him that there was no way that he could've written such an in depth, interesting review. At first Isaac-his name is Isaac by the way- protested and told her that it was his work, and that he hadn't taken it from anyone or anywhere else. She told him not to be disrespectful in class, and she sent him to the principal's office for insubordination. His parents were called. They are *old school* and believe that teachers deserve the utmost of respect, and that their son had been in the wrong for questioning her authority. So he not only got reprimanded at school, but also at home."

"Tough break, but how're you so sure that he didn't copy?"

Renée shook her shoulders. "Aren't there times that you just get a feeling, a hunch, and you're usually right about it?"

"Yeah," Seth said nodding his head in agreement. "It just stinks for Isaac that his attitude towards adults has changed so much just because of one bad experience."

"I know, and I don't know what I can do for him. I'm hoping that eventually he'll let it go. Maybe he will next year when he has a different teacher. But for now, he has a chip on his shoulder. It really bothers me."

"Well, the positive thing is at least he trusted *you*."

Renée considered that for a moment. "True, but it still bothers me. Any suggestions about what to do?"

"Well, I guess just continue what you're doing. I mean, be there for him. Show him that you trust him even if another adult has let him down. It's just a big bummer that his parents aren't backing him on this, you know?" Seth thought of his own father and how he had always jumped to the conclusion, no matter whose fault it had been, that Seth had always been in the wrong. Letting go of that memory, he continued, "You know, I believe that students should definitely have respect for their teachers, and it's unfortunate that a lot of them don't because that's just wrong. But I also feel that sometimes teachers abuse their authority. Right or wrong, that's what I think anyway. Hopefully

Isaac will come around. And due to the fact that you care so much about him, I think he will."

"I hope you're right."

Seth and Renée were in the middle of another discussion when Maggie popped her head out of the doorway. "You guys out here again? What's on the agenda for tonight? Are you devising a solar powered car so we don't have to pay such high gas prices?" She laughed at her comment as she sat down between them.

"Oh, Maggie, would you like to join us?" Seth asked overly politely as he started to smile. "And no, we're not trying to create a solar car. We're talking about the car that has recently been devised that runs purely on water."

"Really?" Maggie exclaimed extremely surprised. "There's really such a car?"

"No!" Seth laughed at her gullibility. "Actually, we were talking about you."

"You were?" Maggie asked even more surprised.

"No, not really," Seth said laughing again as he glanced at Renée, "but it sounded good. Didn't it?"

"Very funny," Maggie said crossing her arms in front of her while pouting.

"What's up, Mags?" Renée asked.

"Well, I was wondering if the two of you were busy tomorrow after you get done with work."

"Not, really," Renée replied. "Why? What did you have in mind?"

"Me neither," Seth answered.

"Well, I was wondering if you guys would like to go with me to look at wedding dresses. If you don't want to come, I totally understand. It's not that big of a deal."

"Not that big of a deal?" Renée almost yelled. "What! Did you set a date without telling us? Of course I'd love to go with you! This is so exciting Maggie." She wrapped her arms around Maggie's neck and gave her a quick hug.

"Thanks, Renée. No, we didn't set a date yet, but I

thought it would be fun to look."

Seth looked slightly confused. "Uh, why would you want me to come along?"

"Oh, come on, Seth. Don't play that game with me. Out of any guy I know, or girl for that matter, you've the best sense of fashion. More importantly, you're so honest that you'd tell me the truth about any dress I try on."

"Thanks, I think." Seth said with uncertainty.

"Oh, Seth, don't worry, your tough guy façade is safe with us." Maggie looked at Renée and smiled. "We both know that underneath that tough exterior that you're a sensitive, understanding, wonderful man. We won't blow your cover."

Renée was laughing at Seth's expression. He just looked at her, rolled his eyes, got up, and explained, "I think I need to go sit on the couch, guzzle some beer, and belch really long and loud."

"Oh, whatever!" Maggie squealed as she grabbed his pant leg. "Set your butt back down here. I didn't mean to offend you. You're just-I don't know- different. But in a good way," she added quickly sensing Seth's embarrassment. "Right, Renée?"

"You are, Seth," Renée said sincerely looking into Seth's eyes and added quietly, "and that's one of the things that I've really come to admire about you."

The next afternoon after Maggie, Renée, and Seth got home from work, the three of them boarded Seth's Camaro and headed to one of the dress shops on Maggie's list. Seth, still uncertain of his participation in this group *outing*, laughed nervously as he parked the car. "Okay, girls," he said mimicking a cheerleader, "ready? Let's go!"

"Oh, come on, Seth!" Maggie pleaded laughing at him. "Won't you *try* and take this seriously? Come on, it's not every day that I'm going to go out and search for a wedding dress."

"Search?" Seth grabbed for his throat as if he were

choking. "Ah, you're killing me Mags. Just how long are we going to *search* for this dress?"

Maggie hurriedly entered the store calling over her shoulder for Seth and Renée to hurry up. Seth and Renée were in no rush as they laughed and joked with each other, taking their time. Finally, deciding to join Maggie in her quest for the perfect dress, Seth dramatically pushed the door open, bowed, and said to Renée, "After you, my lady."

Inside the store, a thin lady with glasses and straight brown hair walked towards them. Seth quickly averted her by becoming overly preoccupied with a suit one of the manikins was wearing. His diversion went undetected as the lady approached him and asked in a friendly voice, "May I help you?"

"No. No, thank you. I'm just looking," Seth said nervously as he looked around the room for Maggie and Renée.

"Oh, it's definitely a big time in your life, isn't it?" she happily questioned, oblivious to the fact that Seth was not the one getting married. Before he had a chance to relay this information to her, she continued, "But it seems like the two of you are definitely going to make it."

"Huh?" Seth asked, confusion written all over his face.

"Oh, I'm sorry. Am I being too bold? I didn't mean to overstep any lines. It's just that we get so many couples who come in together, and there are many times I wonder how long their relationship will last. I don't mean to sound over confident in making this observation, but when I saw the two of you walk in through the door together, it was so evident."

"What was so evident?" Seth asked still confused.

"That the two of you will be together for a long, long time of course," she smiled as she adjusted the tie on the manikin. "You obviously have a million things on your mind, but if you need any assistance, please let me know."

As she walked away, Seth felt his face growing red

from embarrassment. It finally dawned on him that the lady was making reference to him and Renée.

"Having fun yet?" Maggie asked as she walked up behind Seth and tapped him on the shoulder. As he turned around, Maggie noticed how red his face was. "What's wrong with you? Seth, did you say something to the saleslady? Seth, you look embarrassed! What happened?"

"Nothing," Seth added. Trying to quickly change the subject he asked, "So are we done here yet? Do you want to go to another shop?"

"Yeah, I suppose," Maggie said disappointedly. "I've in my mind exactly the kind of dress I want, and I'm just not finding it here."

"So we get to go home?" Seth asked hopefully.

"Nope. Renée, let's go," Maggie said walking towards her. Renée was struggling through a rack of dresses. When she looked up, she almost took Seth's breath away. He didn't know if it was the taffeta and lace surrounding her or the look of determination as she sized up each dress before moving onto the next. Seth turned around trying to disregard the feelings that were again arising and almost choking him, but it was too late. The butterflies quickly took over, and he knew without any doubt in his mind that the feeling he felt was not a figment of his imagination; it was real. He knew he could no longer deny the fact that he had completely and totally fallen in love with Renée.

Shop after shop, Maggie, Renée, and Seth were in pursuit of the perfect dress. The girls rummaged through rack after rack while Seth discreetly tried to keep his distance. He did not want to say anything that would alert Renée to what he was thinking or how he was feeling. To Seth's satisfaction, it appeared to be working. Renée seemed to be caught up in a world of her own.

Driving to another shop on the list, Seth firmly stated, "This is it. I'm tired, hungry, and sick of looking at dresses.

Mags, if you can't find a dress at this shop, let's call it a day. You have time. Your wedding date isn't even set. You can always go looking another day."

Sighing, Maggie replied, "You're right, Seth. It has been a long day. I just don't think I'm going to find the dress I'm looking for. Last shop though before we go home, okay?"

Just steps into the shop, Maggie stopped, grabbed Renée's arm, pointed, and mouthed, "Look!"

Maggie dropped Renée's hand, ran towards the manikin, and stood in awe of the beautiful dress before her. Renée and Seth looked at each other and smiled. "I think she finally found it," Renée said with relief in her voice.

"'Bout time," Seth said, rolling his eyes. Then he questioned, "Just how do I get myself into these things?"

"Well," Renée answered sweetly, "you're a generous, wonderful man who cares about the happiness of others."

"That's the way you see me?" Seth toyed with her. "Well, you couldn't be more wrong. See, my ulterior motive to come along was to get a free meal out of the deal, and I haven't even been successful at that."

"Sure," Renée laughed as she walked to where Maggie was standing in awe by the manikin.

"Well? Should I try it on?" Maggie asked Seth and Renée excitedly. "What do you think?"

"Absolutely," Renée said. "Maggie, there's no doubt in my mind that this is the dress."

In the dressing room, Renée tried to suppress the tears that were forming in her eyes. (*Oh, not now.*) She quickly turned her attention to fussing with the lace on the bottom of Maggie's dress, so that Maggie would not see that she was crying. Although this was an extremely happy time for Maggie, Renée's mind had been drifting to thoughts of her own wedding plans, or more accurately, lack of them. The more she thought about it, the more she realized it was never going to happen- she and Mel were never going to get married. She had known it for a while, but she had thought, believed, and hoped that maybe things would change. Maybe events would take a turn for the better, but she concluded that the likelihood of that happening was slim to none. She helped Maggie pull the dress over her head and zipped it. When Maggie turned around, Renée could no longer keep the tears from spilling from her eyes and down her cheeks.

"Oh, Maggie," Renée gasped as she brought her hands to her cheeks in a gesture of *ah*. "Maggie, you look absolutely stunning. Oh, my gosh. You look so beautiful."

Maggie, with tears in her eyes, turned to look at herself in the mirror. "Oh," was all she could say. She smoothed out the dress, turned to Renée, and asked in a whisper, "Oh, Renée, this is the dress I've always dreamed of. Oh, Renée, it's absolutely perfect. Let's show Seth."

Opening the dressing room door, tears still wet on her cheeks, Renée caught Seth's attention. Waving her hand, she motioned for him to come to the dressing room.

When Maggie came out, even he was speechless. Finally, after a few moments, he said, "Maggie, you look just like a princess." He stepped closer to her, grabbed her hands, and lifted them so he could see the dress more closely. "Mags," he said matter-of-fact, "you should really get this dress." He glanced at Renée who was standing behind them. Tears were still spilling down her cheeks. (*Are those tears of joy or sadness*? Seth wondered.) He briefly imagined what Renée would look like in that dress, and then he quickly dismissed the thought and turned towards Maggie who was asking him a question.

". . . well?" Maggie asked placing her hands on her hips. "What'd you think?"

"Sorry," Seth said embarrassedly. "I was so captivated by how beautiful you look that I didn't even hear what you said."

Maggie started laughing. "All right, Seth, with a comment like that, you're forgiven for not listening. So, I'll ask you again. What do you think of the idea of Joe and me eloping?

"Seriously?" Seth asked confusedly. "You're kidding, right?" Disgusted, he remembered the comment Mel had made. Mel had told him he wanted to elope, so they could just have a big party. At that point, it had become very apparent to Seth that Mel was not interesting in being married, but instead was just interested in his dad paying for a getaway in Vegas, nothing else.

Renée looked from Maggie to Seth and back to Maggie again. "Oh, Maggie, don't you want a wedding where all your friends and family can join you in celebrating? I don't want to sound like an old prude, Mags, but I read somewhere that a wedding is a day, a marriage is a lifetime. Wouldn't you want to start your lifetime together with all the people who honestly love and care about you so much? Mags, you're going to do what you're going to do, but honestly, I think you'd really regret it if you made the decision to elope."

"Okay, okay, you guys!" Maggie said throwing up her arms in a gesture of surrender. "It's not like we booked the airline tickers or anything! We just talked about it the other night, and I wanted to find out how you guys felt about it. I guess I'm glad I did!"

Seth and Renée looked at each other and smiled.

After setting up a payment plan and leaving the store, Seth, Maggie, and Renée all decided it was definitely time to get something to eat. It had been a long, but rewarding afternoon, and all of them were extremely hungry and tired. Joe's Place was still a work in progress. So they decided on a Chinese restaurant.

As they were being shown to their table, Seth suddenly tensed up and became noticeably uncomfortable. Renée glanced ahead of them to a table at which sat two blonde women. One casually turned toward them, and Renée realized it was Kathy. Renée slowed down, grabbed Seth's arm, and whispered quietly, "Uh, Seth, we can go eat somewhere else if you'd like."

Seth shook his head. "Why? Are you afraid that I'm going to make a scene or something?" He took a deep breath, winked, smiled at Renée, and added, "Don't worry. I'll try to behave myself."

"It's not you I'm worried about," Renée said under her breath as she let go of Seth's arm as he, Maggie, and herself followed the hostess to a table by the window.

"This okay?" the hostess, a petite Oriental woman, asked nodding her head. "You want drinks?"

"Yeah, lots of them," Seth mumbled.

"Wha?" the hostess questioned. Not understanding the meaning of Seth's comment, she said, "Your server be right out." As she turned and walked away, Maggie, Seth, and Renée took their places at the table.

"Oh, my gosh!" Maggie complained oblivious to what had just transpired. "I'm so hungry, but before I eat, I really have to go to the bathroom. Renée, come on. Let's go."

"What, does she need to hold your hand?" Seth asked laughing. "You know I've never understood why women can't go to the bathroom by themselves."

"Well, Seth, you can totally join us if you want," Maggie said with mock sincerity.

"No, thanks. I'll pass," he said as he opened his menu. "Hurry up, will you? I'm starving." He smiled and shook his head as Renée and Maggie walked towards the restroom.

Seth was busily looking over the menu, trying to decide on what he would like to eat. He could barely decipher what each item was, as all the wording began to look the same. He did not even notice when Kathy got up from her table and nonchalantly walked over. She brushed her long, blonde hair from her face as she quietly sat down in the chair across from him. "Aren't you going to even say hi?" Kathy asked seductively as she leaned over the table and stared at Seth.

"Uh, hi," Seth answered, annoyed, as he briefly glanced up from his menu. He looked down and added, "What do you want, Kathy? I'm kind of busy right now."

"So I see," she answered rolling her eyes. "It didn't take you long to move on."

Seth closed his menu, folded his hands in front of him and asked very pointedly, "And what exactly is *that* supposed to mean?"

"Oh, come on, Seth," she replied in a frustrated tone. "What? Do you think I'm that stupid? You and I get into a little fight, you move out, and the next thing I know you're living with little *Miss Thing*."

"Her name is Renée," Seth replied calmly, "and I'm not *living* with her."

"Yeah, well, call it whatever you want, Seth, but it's pretty obvious what's going on."

"Listen, Kathy," Seth said slowly running out of patience, "why don't you go back to your table, finish your dinner, and leave me alone. Okay?"

"You're asking me to leave?" Kathy inquired in disbelief. Seth ignored her as he picked up his menu and again began to study it. Upset with his actions, she sucked in a heated breath and quietly hissed, "Fine, Seth. Fine."

As Kathy was angrily returning to her table, she passed by Renée and Maggie walking back from the restroom. She stopped, looked Renée up and down, and remarked with disgust, "You know, you don't even have a chance with him. You're *definitely* not his type."

"Go away," Maggie said turning around and rudely waving her hand in front of Kathy's face. "Something's starting to stink around here, and I'm pretty sure it's you."

Kathy glared at Maggie. Before she stomped back to her table, she turned one last time and factually called after

Renée, "You know, you're nothing to him. He's just using you. When he gets tired of slumming, he'll come back to me. You just wait and see."

"I'm gonna kill that little bitch," Maggie said under her breath as she turned around and headed in Kathy's direction.

Renée grabbed her by the arm and turned her around. "It's not worth it, Mags, just let it go. Don't you think it's enough punishment for her to wake up with herself every morning?"

Maggie stopped, stared at Renée, and started laughing. "Renée, you're just too good to be true. Okay, okay. You're right. She's not worth my time. And besides, I'm hungry. Let's get back to the table so we can order."

That night when Seth, Renée, and Maggie returned from their shopping adventure, Mel was sitting at the dining room table. He looked up from his sandwich and glared at the three of them as they tiredly walked through the door into the entryway.

"I'm going to bed. I'm exhausted," Maggie said with a yawn as she gave Renée a hug. "Thank you, oh, thank you, Renée, for everything," she whispered holding onto her tightly. "It was the best time ever." She turned around, unaware of Mel's callous look, as she walked down the hallway humming softly a wedding march. Moving as if she were floating on a cloud, she opened the door and went upstairs.

Seemingly captivated by Maggie's happiness, Seth appeared unaware of Mel's obvious scowl. "I think I'm going to watch some TV and then go to bed. Good night. It was fun today," he added as he went to the basement door, opened it, and walked downstairs.

"So," Mel finally asked in a rancorous tone as he idly played with the potato chips on his plate, "you were out again without me?"

"Mel, it wasn't like that," Renée tried to explain as she attempted to rub Mel's shoulders while he was sitting in his chair. "Maggie asked us if we wanted to come with her to pick out a wedding dress. I didn't even think to ask you if you wanted to come. Because you've been working a lot lately, I figured you'd be busy."

Mel brushed her arms off his shoulders as he abruptly stood up from the table. "Yeah, I suppose now that Maggie's having this big *whoop de doo* wedding that's what you're gonna want too." He looked at her disgustedly. "Well, Renée, I've news for you. I've been giving a lot of thought to our wedding. I'm thinking that either we elope, or we just forget about it." He stared at her waiting for a response. "What? Now you're not gonna answer me?" He unexpectedly slammed his hand on the table, and the plate of uneaten chips and his sandwich went flying to the floor.

Renée absent-mindedly bent down and began picking up what was left of the food. She heaved a sigh and began putting it back on the plate.

"And yeah, that's another thing, Renée," he said as he bent down beside her, "isn't a good fiancé usually home to make supper? Look at the crap I had to eat because you weren't here to make anything."

"Mel..."

"I don't even want to hear it," he remarked as he infuriatingly got to his feet, throwing his arms into the air. As he stomped away, he remarked over his shoulder, "I'm going out. Don't even bother waiting up for me." He slammed the door as he left the house. Renée heard his car start and roar out of the driveway.

(*Not again.*) She placed the half eaten plate of food on the table and sat in the chair in which Mel had been sitting. She folded her arms on the table, laid her head on top of them, and let the tears fall. (*I have to find a way out of this and soon. I can't live like this... no, I won't live like this.*)

# Chapter VII

As the days passed, Maggie, Seth, and Renée became inseparable. Any uncertainties or insecurities Renée had about sharing her home with two people she really didn't know that well had quickly disappeared. It was as if the three of them had known each other all their lives. Renée could not remember a time when she felt as secure and happy. A confidence was growing inside her, and it was something that made her feel alive, yet hesitant. She was beginning to, for the first time in her life, feel that she deserved more, was worth more, and because of this, she knew she would have to make some difficult decisions in regards to her future.

"So," Renée said as she took a sip of her strawberry shake, "when are the two of you going to move out and find your own places to live?" It was Saturday, the middle of July. Seth, Maggie, and Renée were relaxing from the hectic work week on a blanket by the river, watching the ducks stroll around the edge. Some of them were venturing so close that Seth threw the top half of his hamburger bun in a feeble attempt to scare them away.

"You dork!" Maggie said as she kicked at Seth's leg. "Now they're going to want all of our food. I work hard during the week so I can enjoy my ice-cream treat on the weekend, and I don't want to share it with some dumb ducks!"

Renée playfully flicked some ice-cream at Seth. "Yeah, way to go, you dork!"

"Oh, my God," Seth said, trying to look as annoyed as possible, "you would think the two of you were twelve instead of twenty-five. Come on, grow up!" he said teasingly as he rolled his eyes at them. He got up, walked to the picnic table, sat down, and pretended to be upset.

"Seriously, guys," Renée said as she got up and took a seat next to Seth, ignoring his pretend pouting, "how long do you think you guys will stay?"

Seth looked intently into Renee's eyes, and instead of a comical answer to which she was accustomed, he said, "As long as it takes."

Renée turned away and suddenly pretended to be very interested in the ducks that, in spite of a hamburger bun being flung at their heads, were bravely approaching the table.

Maggie got up from the blanket, kicked at the ducks that were in her path, and sat across the table from Renée. "Listen, Renée, Seth and I've been talking." Renée looked from Seth to Maggie and back to Seth again. She held her breath, prepared for the inevitable truth Maggie was about to speak. "There's really no easy way to say this, and I'm not going to sugar coat it, so here goes . . . your fiancé is a jerk. He is, Renée, and Seth and I don't want to leave until we're sure that you're going to be okay. That's honestly why we're staying. I mean come on, Renée. You've seen the way that the business at my shop has been picking up. I have colors, highlights, and cuts scheduled from now until after Labor Day. Initially, this was going to be a temporary stay for me, you know? My last apartment sucked, and you gave me a place to crash until I could find another one. Well, to tell you the truth, I haven't really been looking all that hard. I *like* staying at the house with you and Seth. This might sound odd, but in this short amount of time, the two of you have become like family."

Seth cleared his throat, but without looking up he said, "Yeah, I know what you mean."

Maggie continued, "If you want me out, if that's what this is leading to, worst case scenario, I could crash at Joe's for a while. I don't know that he would mind. I realize it might sound old-fashioned and stuff that we didn't want to live together until we're married, but. . ."

"No, no, Maggie," Renée softly broke in without giving Maggie the chance to finish her sentence, "it's just that . . . it's just that. . ." Renée tried to finish her sentence, but tears began to stream down her face. She quickly wiped them away annoyed with herself that she was crying yet again. She took a deep breath and continued, "I want to leave *him*, but I just don't know how. I'm scared."

Seth gently put his arm around Renée's shoulders. "It'll be okay. I promise. Maggie and I'll help you."

"Of course," Maggie said in all seriousness. "Of course we will." Then she sat back with a big smile on her face. "Hey, Seth, maybe you could falsify some documents and get that son-of-a-bitch thrown in jail!" she said delighted by her sudden stroke of genius.

"Maggie," Seth said as he looked at her, shaking his head from side to side, trying to suppress a smile, "I'm a probation officer. Just what documents do you foresee me falsifying?"

"Whatever, it was just a thought," Maggie said as she annoyingly swatted at a fly that was circling around the ice-cream on the tip of her nose. In doing so, she comically crossed her eyes.

Renée, watching Maggie attack the fly, could not contain her laughter. The harder she tried to stop, the more difficult it became. "Oh, Maggie, you're too much," she was finally able to say between giggles.

"Yeah? That's funny, because that's what Joe always says," she casually commented raising her eyebrows. She smugly smiled and continued, "But enough about that. Let's get serious. What finally changed your mind about Mel?"

"I don't know, Maggie, I guess I finally got to the point of being sick and tired of being sick and tired. Have you ever wanted something so badly that you didn't realize that it was killing you?"

Seth and Maggie each gave her a confused, concerned look.

"Okay, let me back up," Renée said as she wiped the tears from her face and tucked a loose strand of hair behind her ear. "You both know that I don't have the best relationship with my family, that I've always felt like I was the oddball. Like I was a square peg trying to fit into a round hole."

"Yeah," Seth said, "continue."

"Well, anyway, believe it or not, when I first met Mel, he made me feel like I was- I don't know- special. The beginning of our relationship was wonderful. He was kind, courteous, and he treated me with respect. . ."

"So this changed when?" Maggie quickly interrupted. She wanted to say more, but Seth shot her a look, and she kept her comments to herself.

"It didn't change right away, just gradually. So I just assumed that it was something I had said or done that . . . this sounds so juvenile," Renée said covering her face with her fingers. She slowly put them down and continued, "I thought it was my fault that the relationship had gone bad. Do either of you have any idea what I'm talking about?"

"Yeah, I do," Seth said. "Anyway, I think I do. I always felt like an outsider in my family, too. Like with my dad, no matter what I did, it wasn't good enough. I got to the point that I thought I deserved the bad breaks in life. It sucks. It really does. I always felt like my family didn't care about me, so why would anyone else? Because of that, I wasn't very selective about who I dated. It sounds pathetic, but I dated whoever I thought would put up with the all-out-loser I had believed myself to be."

"Huh? Really?" Maggie unbelievingly asked Seth. "You felt that way? God, Seth, I'm the one who feels like a loser now. I've known you for years. Why didn't you ever tell me any of this?"

"Ah, what was I supposed to say, Maggie? Hi, I'm Seth, and I have low self-esteem and am an insecure, pathetic soul because my family didn't include me and treated me like an outcast? Yeah, you're right," he said with a smile, "that's exactly what I should've told you."

"Whatever!" Maggie squealed in a high-pitched voice as she punched Seth's shoulder.

"Ouch," Seth said with mock superiority, "that really hurt, Maggie." Then they both became quiet in an attempt to give Renée an opportunity to continue.

Renée nervously glanced from Seth to Maggie and then to Seth again before she pensively went on, "I know I need to leave him, but what do I do? I don't even know where to start. I feel like I'm dragging the two of you into this, and it's hard to ask for help. You know? I've always felt like if I got myself into something, I should be able to get myself out. But this time, I know I can't."

"Renée," Seth said with all earnestly, "we're here to help you in anyway we can."

Renée let out a deep breath as she tucked her hair behind her ears. "I need a plan. I need to figure out what my next step is going to be."

"I could shoot him," Maggie said with a smile.

"Yeah, that'll solve everything," observed Seth as he rolled his eyes. "Apparently, this is something you haven't just decided overnight, so what had been holding you back?"

Renée looked at Seth. "Seth, I've always tried to see the good in people, you know? I guess I'm kind of a pathetic excuse for a Pollyanna, but I've always believed that if I gave people chances when other people turned their backs on them, that I could somehow make a difference."

"So you felt sorry for Mel?" Maggie interjected with a confused look.

"No, not exactly. Deep down I believe Mel *is* a really good man. As difficult as it may be for the two of you to understand, that's the man I fell in love with. It's almost like he has a split personality or something. I believe he wants to do the right thing and be a good person, but it's as if something's holding him back."

"And you got to the point that you were sick and tired of making excuses for his behavior, and you've come to the realization that no matter how much you do for him, care for him, love him, he won't change until he's ready," Seth said as if he were recalling a memory from his past rather then speaking of Renée's present situation. "Yeah, I can relate. You know this isn't going to be easy. You know that when you do tell Mel that it's over, he's going to try everything he can to try and get you to change your mind. And if you decide to take him back, he will, in all likelihood, treat you well for a while. But then you know he'll go back to the way he used to be."

"It sounds like a vicious cycle," Maggie stated.

"It is," continued Seth. "It's the cycle of abuse. You know that abuse doesn't necessarily have to be physical. It can be verbal, mental, or psychological . . . there're all kinds of abuse. But they're all abuse just the same. You understand this, right?"

Renée took a deep breath, sighed, and said, "I know."

"And," Maggie added, "you also know that this is *not* your fault, and you didn't do anything to cause it, right?"

She looked Renee square in the eyes before continuing. "Renée, you're a beautiful, intelligent, outgoing, and caring woman. You've so much going for you. What're you afraid of?"

Renée looked at her. "It's a lot of things. . ."

"We're here for you, Renée," Seth coaxed. "Please talk to us."

"I'm afraid of being alone. . . I'm afraid that this is my last chance at having the husband, family, home, dog- the *American dream*. If I don't take it, I won't have another chance. I turned thirty this past April and my biological clock *is* ticking." She stifled a smile through her tears. "I hate that saying, you know? But it's more than that. After college, I moved away from home, and I thought I would really do something with my life. I thought things would just kind of fall into place, but you know the old saying *wherever you go, there you are. . .* As much as I tried to push the insecurities of my past relationships, especially with my family, away, they would still resurface. I would have thoughts like 'I'm not good enough to be doing this' or 'Things will never work out anyway' and so on. As hopelessly pathetic as this sounds, I've always been hoping that there would be that special someone who I could share my life with. Either I've missed him along the way, or he's never going to be there, I just don't know."

Seth dared not look up. He had made a promise to himself that although difficult, he was going to maintain nothing more than a friendship with Renée. But her candor, her honesty, her whole demeanor had touched something deep within his being. He had felt it time and time again when he was around her. It was more than a physical attraction, or a fleeting thought that would eventually dissipate. She truly was the one for whom he had been praying.

# Chapter VIII

"What?" Maggie confusedly asked. "You're really *thirty*? Wow, you're sooooooooo old!"

"Oh, be quiet, Maggie," Renée said with a smile. "Yes, you guys just *assumed* I was twenty-five. Who was I to dispute your incorrect thinking?"

Seth laughed. "Okay, now that that trivial piece of evidence is uncovered, can we continue with our conversation?"

"Seth, you are such a . . . such a. . ."

"Dork?" Renée playfully added.

"Yeah," Maggie agreed with a grin.

"What're you going to do about the house?" Seth asked off-handedly, pretending to be interested in a boat on the river, not yet ready to look into Renée's eyes.

"I don't know. You asked me what I'm scared of, and that's another thing. As odd as it sounds, I thought that when we got the house, that it would bring Mel and I closer together." She shrugged her shoulders and mused, "I really don't know why. Instead, all it's turned out to be is a huge financial burden."

Seth and Maggie looked across the table at each other. "Renée," Maggie said, "Seth and I *can* find somewhere else to stay. You know you *can* sell it."

"Oh, I didn't mean it that way. I know that the only reason the two of you have stayed as long as you have is because you care so much about me." She let out a slight laugh and with pain in her eyes admitted, "I'm worried about being able to get Mel to leave. It's almost like he thinks that if he can keep the house, he somehow will be able to keep me. Weird, don't you think? But that's how it is. I've, believe it or not, talked with him about selling it. When I do, he says things like 'Good luck, I'm not gonna help you' or 'Good luck selling it when I'm still living here 'cause I'm not leaving'. I guess it depends on his mood at the time. Seth, I know you're not a lawyer, but don't you know someone who I could talk to about this?"

"Yeah, you're right. I don't know a lot about the legalities, but I'll do my best to find someone who does."

"Tell the son-of-a-bitch that he has to leave," Maggie rudely remarked.

"Yeah, I wish it were that easy," Renée commented quietly.

After her luncheon by the river with Maggie and Seth, Renée felt hopeful, tired but hopeful. It had been an emotionally exhausting afternoon. Although Seth and Maggie had offered to come with her when she talked with Mel, she knew it was something that she had to do on her own. As she turned onto their street and saw that Mel's vehicle was parked in the driveway in his self-assigned *spot*, unease crept into her stomach. The past few days she and Mel had barely spoken, partly because Mel had been working odd, sometimes unusually late hours, and partly because when he was home, he was too engrossed in his video games to acknowledge that she was in the same room with him.

She turned off the engine and sat in her car. She was trying to get up enough nerve to walk in the house and tell Mel that it was over. Taking a deep breath, grasping the steering wheel, she rehearsed in her head what she planned to tell him. Finally, feeling like she was ready, she reached for the door handle. However, in the side of the door, she noticed a picture. She picked it up. As her eyes filled with tears, she looked at Mel and herself smiling back at her. It was one of the first pictures they had taken together when their relationship was new, and the two of them appeared to be so in love. She stared at the picture and whispered, "Oh, Mel, how could things have changed so much?" She let the picture fall from her fingertips as she her mind drifted back to the day they had first met.

\* \* \*

It had been a Saturday afternoon. Renée had spent the morning looking for a birthday present for her sister. She had been anything but enthused about the task due to the fact that shopping had never been one of her favorite pastimes. The pressure of wanting to buy something, but not knowing exactly what it would be, had not helped to make the situation any more pleasurable. She had woken up early and had gotten to the mall as the stores were beginning to open in hopes of avoiding the crowd of afternoon shoppers. She had wandered from shop to shop, but nothing had really caught her eye. The stores had become more and more crowded. So annoyed, frustrated, and hungry, she had resolved to skip the gift buying and go home. The thought of sending her sister a card with a gift card enclosed had seemed to be the most appealing idea.

She had exited through the doors of the mall's main entrance and had proceeded to look for where she had parked her car. Of course, it was not where she had thought she had left it. In frustration, she had continued to look until finally she had recognized the license plate of her four-door, red car- unfortunately a popular color for cars in that parking lot. Walking towards it, she had seen a man with a look of dismay on his face standing by a car that had a flat tire with a spare propped up next to a car beside him.

Renée had unlocked her door and had been getting in the car when something had made her look back at the man. "Oh, my gosh," she had said with pity and surprise, "the poor guy doesn't know the first thing about changing a tire." Although she had recognized the fact that it might be a bit risky helping a complete stranger, she had ignored her gut feeling, had gotten out of her car, and had walked to where the man was parked.

"Uh, hi," he had said smiling with a boyish grin as he held the jack in one hand and the tire iron in the other.

"Uh, hi," Renee had smiled. "Do you need some help?" He had looked so perplexed that the expression on his face had appeared almost comical.

"Well," he had scratched his head after setting down the jack, "I know I *should* know how to change this, but," he had laughed as he had shrugged his shoulders in disbelief. "I honestly don't know how."

"Hmmmm," Renée had commented as she smiled at his obvious lack of mechanical aptitude. "Here, give me the jack."

He had obligingly handed it to her and watched as she had secured it and had begun jacking up the car. "The first thing we have to do is get the tire off. Uh, you *do* have a spare, right?" Of course Renée already knew the answer. She had seen it propped up to the car next to them, but she was trying to make polite conversation.

He had looked at her and stated proudly, "Yup, I already got that out of the trunk. It's right there." He had pointed to a donut tire leaning against the car parked next to him.

After completing the task of changing the tire, Renée

had wiped her hands on her jeans, and said, "There you go."

As she had been turning to leave, he had said, "Hey, hey, wait a minute." He had held out his hand and stated, "I'm Mel."

Renée had shaken his hand, smiled, and had replied, "Renée."

"Otherwise known as an angel in disguise?" He had looked her in the eyes and added, "All I have to say is that if all the angels in heaven are as beautiful as you, I better get my act together because that's where I'll be wanting to spend my time."

Renée had blushed and smiled. "Thanks."

As she had turned again to walk back to her car, Mel had, in a desperate attempt to continue the conversation, almost hollered, "Hey, wait. Are you in a hurry? I mean, I know this is kind of forward, but the least I could do is take you out to eat or for coffee or something."

Renée had taken a deep breath. He was cute. She had to give him that, but the last thing she wanted was to get involved with someone romantically. It had been only three months since Jack had walked out of her life, and she did not feel she was ready for any kind of relationship for quite a while. She still clung to the hope that the two of them might reconcile. As time passed, the chance of that seemed to be slimmer and slimmer. He had broken her heart, and the idea of letting someone else fill the deep hole he had created seemed unfathomable. "Uh, I don't think so, but thanks."

Mel had been unwilling to give up so easily. He had reverted to what he had come to know would work in times past when he saw something he had wanted, and he wasn't able to get it . . . manipulation. "Well, I'm so sorry to hear that. I'm really hungry, and I was so hoping that someone as lovely and interesting as yourself would come with me to a new restaurant that I really want to try." He had looked at her, given her his best smile, and had added in a pleading almost childlike tone, "Please?"

Looking back, Renée knew the answer should have been a simple no. She should have resolved to turn and walk away. However, something about the way he had talked to her, looked at her, had caught her off guard. She had found herself feeling powerless over his relentless persuasion. "Okay, okay. Where is this restaurant?"

As an expression of his excitement, Renée had thought he was going to grab her and give her a hug. Instead, he had almost too excitedly replied, "Get in your car and follow me."

\* \* \*

Brushing the memory aside, she crumpled the picture which she was still holding and threw it in the trashcan by the garage. She steadied herself, and with as much confidence as she was able to gather, walked solemnly to the house. "Well, it's now or never," she whispered as she placed her hand on the doorknob and gently opened the door.

The music was blaring so loudly, that Renée was surprised that Mel could hear anything as he was talking on the phone. While she waited for him to finish his conversation, she scooped up Tyon, petted him, and let him loose in the back yard. When she came back into the house, Mel was saying, "Uh, yeah. I know where the place is. Yeah, a pick up tonight?" Mel put his hand over the receiver of the phone as he saw Renée. He pointed to the clock and mouthed 'Where were you?' He gave Renée a disgusted look and then speaking into the phone said, "I'll have to call you back. Don't worry, I'll be there."

"Hi," Renée said as Mel angrily walked to their bedroom. "Do you have some time? We really need to talk."

"Uh, not right now," Mel said as he came out of the

bedroom zipping the zipper of his jeans, and then he bent down to fasten the strap on his sandal. "We were supposed to be at my dad's an hour ago. Where the hell were you?"

"Oh, no, I completely forgot," Renée said as Mel glared at her. Then she calmly asked, "Are we still going?"

"Well, duh?" Mel said rolling his eyes in disbelief at what he considered her obviously brainless question. "Are you ready?"

"Um..."

"Oh, don't even do this, Renée. Don't give me some feeble excuse why you don't want to go. And you still haven't told me where you were." He fidgeted with his watch, "Oh, let me guess, out with Seth?"

Renée desperately tried to remain confident as she calmly answered, "I had lunch with Maggie and Seth by the river. I thought you'd be working. I'm sorry. I really forgot about going out to your dad's."

"Yeah, I'm sure. Blow me off to spend time with your *boyfriend.*"

The way he over enunciated the word boyfriend made her feel guilty as if she had done something wrong. "Why do you keep saying that?" Renée evenly queried. "You know that Seth and I are just friends."

"Do I? Do I really know that, Renée?" Mel hissed barely allowing her to finish her sentence. "You know, Renée, you're a lot of things, but I never took you as a liar and a cheat!" He furiously barked as he hastily began walking towards her.

Moving backwards in an attempt to step away, in a calm voice she tried to reason with him. "Why don't you just go to your dad's yourself, Mel? You're angry, and I don't want us to get into another argument. But when you come home, we really need to talk."

"Why don't you just go to your dad's yourself, Mel?" he mimicked, as he stood as close to her as was possible without allowing his body to come in contact with hers.

"Please, let me by," Renée said as her face was becoming flushed and her palms were beginning to sweat form the nervousness and tension she was feeling. "If you're not going to leave, I am."

"Oh, no, you're not, you little whore!" Mel screamed as he slapped her as hard as he could across the face.

Renée lost her balance, tripped over a chair, and hit the side of her head on the table. When she picked herself off the floor, he came after her again. In desperation, she screamed, "Get out! Get out or I'm calling the cops!"

"Oh, call the cops! Big deal! You're really scaring me, Renée! Maybe it's time I give you a taste of your own medicine!" He shrilly remarked as he proceeded to push past her. He violently turned the table on its side as it barely missed her. It was as if something inside him snapped; like he was no longer in control of his actions. "How do you like that? Or this!" He spit out the words as he threw a book in her direction. If she hadn't ducked, it would have hit her in the face. He then went into the kitchen and grabbed a knife.

"Oh, my God! No, Mel!" she shrieked as she frantically ran to the bathroom, slammed the door, and locked it.

Mel began pounding on the door in an attempt to get Renée to open it. "Come out of there, come out and get what's coming to you, you two-timing whore! Come out or I'll break the God-damned thing down!" He repeatedly slammed his shoulder into it. "You know there's no one who's going to help you! You're nothing, Renée, nothing. Haven't you realized that yet?"

From behind the bathroom door, Renée trembled in fear. She was crying so hard she could barely breathe. She gingerly touched the side of her head that was throbbing with pain, and she felt the blood leak through her fingers. She felt the pockets of her jeans, praying that her cell phone was there, but it wasn't. She tried to stifle her tears and listen if Mel was still in the house. Daring not to move too much from her spot on the bathroom floor, she slowly lifted her head and pressed her ear against the door. Over the screaming music, she could hear the breaking of glass, Mel swearing as he threw objects against the wall, and finally, the sound of the backdoor slamming.

"He's gone," whispered Renée. "Thank you, God, he's gone." She pulled her knees close to her chest, rested her arms on them, and leaned her head against the door and cried. No matter how hard she tried to stop the flow of tears, they kept falling, rolling down her cheeks. She sat in a state of shock, unable to move. She had no idea how much time had passed when she finally felt strong enough to pull herself to her feet and stand up. Standing in front of the bathroom sink, she stared in disbelief at the reflection staring back at her in the mirror. Her eyes were puffy and red. The side of her face that had hit the table was swollen. Already she could see a bruise starting to form. Turning on the faucet, she began splashing cool water on her face. She attempted to wash away the blood, tears, and most of all the fear that was still hanging heavily in the air. Reaching for a towel, she lifted her head and looked up. The image staring at her was more terrifying than anything she could have imagined.

"Bet you thought I was gone for good," sneered Mel, as he brought his fist back to hit her. Renée moved for the bathroom door that she mistakenly thought she had locked. As she did, Mel's fist hit the mirror and it splintered into a hundred web-like pieces. "You dumb whore! Now look at what you did!" Blood was seeping from between his knuckles. "Get back here!" he screamed as he grabbed Renée by the hair just as she made it out the bathroom door into the narrow hallway outside the living room. He threw her on the floor and proceeded to sit on top of her. He pinned her arms to the ground so she was not able to move.

"Let me go! Let me go, Mel! You don't know what you're doing!" Renée screamed, terrifyingly pleading.

It was to no avail as Mel scoffed at her, "Oh, yes I do, you whiny little whore! You're getting exactly what you deserve!" He leaned over her face, so his was just inches above hers and whispered in the most degrading, demeaning tone he could conjure up, "You're nothing but a worthless, dumb bitch. You're a dog. And now, I'm going to beat you like the dog you are, and if you don't shut up, I'm gonna kill you like the dog you are."

Just as Mel raised his arm to strike Renée, Seth caught it. He twisted it behind Mel's back and flung him off of Renée. "Don't you *ever* threaten her," he warned between clenched teeth.

Mel clumsily got to his feet, and cowardly ran behind his large, overstuffed, orange chair at which he usually sat and played video games. "What? What the hell are you doing here?" With the chair between them, Mel cockily said, "Tough guy, huh? Well, come on! Come on you weak, useless bastard, let's see what you got!"

Seth slowly got up, glared at Mel, and informingly stated, "You don't want to start something you can't finish."

Maggie, who had been standing behind Seth, ran to Renée. "Oh, my God, Renée, oh, Renée," she said as she wrapped her arms around her and rocked her back and forth. Maggie and Renée watched in disbelief as Seth's whole demeanor seemed to change before them. His voice, his face, his stance, it was as if he had transformed into an entirely different person. His normally brown eyes, turned almost black, as they peered at Mel in an eerie gaze. His jaw line became more distinct and tight, and his body became loose, almost like a tiger stalking its prey. Not knowing whether to be relieved or terrified, Maggie gently got Renée to her feet and guided her to the opposite side of the room.

"Bring it on, tough guy," Mel taunted, but he too looked alarmed observing the obvious change in Seth. Mel ran for Seth, and before he could land a punch, Seth had him flat on his back.

Seth's fighting maneuvers were ones that Renée had never before witnessed. The intensity and malice with which he attacked Mel frightened her. "Seth!" she screamed and tried to move towards him, but Maggie held her tightly. "Seth! Let him go, or you're going to kill him!"

Renée's words brought Seth back from the trance he seemed to be under. "Get up," he said as he stood away from Mel. Mel was huddled in the corner quietly crying. "Get up!" Seth said again more loudly as he moved towards him.

Mel, shielding his face, slowly crawled to his feet. "I am," he cried as he blubbered like a baby. "Just don't hit me anymore. Don't come near me!"

"Get out of here, now," Seth said taking a deep breath. Looking out of the corner of his eye at Renée he added, "If you ever lay a hand on her again. . ."

Before Seth could finish his sentence, Mel was out the door, in his car, and was driving away.

Seth turned and looked at Renée still huddled in the corner tightly holding onto Maggie. When his and Renée's eyes met, she saw the black disappear from them. Then they returned to the gentle, sincere, brown that Renée had come to know and trust. Even in view of the obvious change to his old self, Renée tentatively clung to Maggie uncertain of this man gently kneeling beside her; the man who had, in all probability, saved her life.

"Renée, oh, Renée," Seth said barely above a whisper as he slowly reached, in fear that he might frighten her, and touched her swollen face. He tenderly held her face in his hands, as his eyes welled up with tears. "Come here, honey." He held her closely to his chest. Tears, with a mixture of blood, fell on his white t-shirt while he gently stroked her hair. As calmly as possible, he tried to console her by saying over and over, "It's going to be okay."

Realizing Renée was going to be alright, Maggie boldly asked, "Where in God's name did you learn to fight like that? I've never seen anything like that except on some funky action movie."

Seth took a deep breath as he felt Renée's arms on his chest pushing him slightly away from her, so she could once again look into his soft, brown eyes. "Yes, Seth," she asked shakily, "how did you learn that?"

Seth, looking down from their intent gazes, finally said, "Well, I wasn't always the person I am today." He stopped, wiped his eyes, and regained his composure. "Before finally getting my act together and straightening out my life, I used to hang with some pretty shady characters." He looked into Renée's questioning eyes and continued, "I've done some pretty messed up things in my life, things I'm not too proud of. Like I said, I used to be a completely different person."

"But, Seth, you're nothing like that now. What changed?" Maggie questioned.

"A lot," Seth said. He chose his next words carefully, feeling Renée's uncertainty and fear. "But for the grace of God, there go I."

"What?" Maggie asked with confusion. "You mean to tell us that you went from a thug to this awesome guy because of God?"

"Something like that," Seth answered softly. "There's more to it than that, but let's save that for another day. Okay?"

Renée whispered, "With God, all is possible, right? At least that's what I had believed at one point in my life. But now, well," although she tried as hard as she could to stop them, the tears continued to fall.

"We need to call the cops, Seth," Maggie said looking around the room. It was in shambles. Then she said to Renée, "But first we need to get you to the hospital."

# Chapter IX

"No good whore," Mel swore under his breath. "What the hell was that bitch thinking?" He had stopped at a gas station about a block from where he was supposed to meet his *business associate*, so he could drop off his merchandise. When he went inside to use the restroom, the clerk had given him an odd look. Looking in the small mirror above the sink in the cramped bathroom, Mel could see why. He had a cut above his eyebrow, and although he had done his best to wipe away the blood with his hand, it had dried around his eye which was already beginning to swell shut. He felt in the back of his mouth and pulled out a tooth that had been knocked out by Seth's punch. (*What the hell happened?*) In all the fights in which Mel had been, he had never seen anyone come after him like that. If he would have had any sense, he would have left before Seth had had the chance to land the first punch. However, Mel felt he had had something to prove. No one, no one including Renée, Seth, or anyone was ever going to tell him what to do. He checked his watch, swore under his breath, and commented, "Damn, I'm gonna be late for the pick up."

He left the gas station, got back in his car, and took out his cell phone. "Yeah, it's Mel. Yeah, yeah, I know. I got delayed, and I'm gonna be a little late. Whatever. Do you want me there or not? Alright, bye." Mel hung up the phone, checked from side to side for any unmarked police cars, and then proceeded to drive into an alley. Outside the gas station, a tall, middle-aged man made a call on his cell phone while sitting in his car. "It's a go. He just left, and yeah, the little punk's really in for it now. We just got a report, and there's an A.P.B. out for him. In addition to everything else we got on him, we can also add to the list terroristic threats and domestic abuse."

Mel drove through the alley and parked outside a run down two-story house. By this time, the summer sky was getting dark. He leaned back in his seat, lit a cigarette, and waited. The energy exerted in the fight had taken its toll on him; he was exhausted. He dozed off for what seemed only a minute. When he came to, there was a bright light in his eyes, and he saw a red light flashing in his rear-view mirror.

"Get out of the car," the officer said as he shined his flashlight at him.

"What the . . .?" Mel swore under his breath. "What, I can't park in the alley? What's your problem? You wanna give me a breathalyzer? I'm not drunk."

"Get out of the car," the officer said again with obvious annoyance for having to repeat his statement. Mel didn't move. He sat motionless contemplating what he was going to do. In an attempt of desperation, he hurriedly swung open his car door and slammed it as hard as he could into the body of the officer. He hastily exited the car and began running down the alley.

The force of the door flung the officer to the ground. Grabbing his gun from its holster, he rolled on his side, aimed his gun at Mel, and screamed, "Freeze! Freeze or I'll shoot!" Before Mel could take another step, he was forcefully tackled from the side.

The wind was knocked out of him as he landed on his back. When he finally caught his breath, he sputtered, "What the?"

"Shut-up, you little punk. Get up. You're going downtown," said the man who had been parked outside the gas station making the phone call after Mel had left. He, Jake Benson, was an undercover agent working for the Narcotics Division. He had been tracking Mel, Roger, and their drug ring for some time. Finally, because of Mel's stupidity, he was able to nail him. "You have the right to remain silent, anything you say can and will be held against you; you have the right to an attorney. . ." Jake continued reading Mel his Miranda Rights as he shoved him in the squad car and headed down to the station.

Renée felt like she was in a nightmare, and soon she would wake up and things would go back to normal. (*What happened? What caused Mel to just "snap"?*) There had been times in the past that he had gotten angry and lost his cool, but it had never been as bad as what she had experienced this time. (*Was he high?*) The thought, prior to that moment, had never really occurred to her. She felt naïve and stupid for never considering it although it helped her to comprehend why his behavior might have changed so drastically over the past months.

She was sitting on the couch, staring blankly ahead, and the tears just kept running down her cheeks. "They caught Mel," Seth said as he handed her a cup of tea. She had been checked over and released from the hospital. With the exception of some pretty noticeable bruises, physically, she was going to be okay. Maggie and Seth had stayed by her side as the doctor had examined her. Afterwards, there had been a police officer waiting to talk with her.

Initially, Renée's face had gone white, but she truthfully had answered all of the policeman's questions. Seth had been afraid she was going to faint when he had started asking her about Mel's involvement in a drug ring.

"I don't know. . . I, I," Renée had stammered looking from Maggie to Seth and back to Maggie again.

The policeman had been polite and courteous. In view of all Renée had obviously been through, he did not push the issue. Instead, he had responded, "That's all the information we need from you at this time. We'll be in touch. In the mean time, if you need anything, please give me a call at this number."

Renée had taken his card, tucked it away in her purse, and again began to cry.

"Renée? Renée?" Seth sat down beside her on the brown, soft suede couch. "You're not going to believe the list of charges they have against him. If they all stick, which I believe they will, he's going to be going away for quite some time."

Renée held the tea firmly in one hand, and pulled her blanket up under her chin with the other. "Seth," she said quietly, "if this was the right thing to do, then why do I feel so awful?" She looked at him with such sadness, that Seth could almost feel her pain.

"You *are* a good person, Renée. You always try to see the good in people, but have you ever thought that some people just don't care?"

Renée looked like Seth had punched her in the stomach.

I'm sorry, Renée," Seth said apologetically. "I didn't mean for that to sound so harsh. It's just that there're some people, and no matter how much you love them and care for them, they just never seem to want to see the good in themselves. You can't change that, Renée. You know this, right? You have to know in your heart that if loving someone would be enough, Mel would've changed."

"I know you're right, Seth, but it still hurts. I feel so . . .

so . . . used. I was never anything to him. He lied to me about everything, even about loving me."

"Have you ever considered that some people just don't know how to love?"

Renée pondered this idea for a few moments. Then peering absent-minded into her teacup she answered, "I guess I never thought about it that way." She heavily sighed and asked, "But what do I do now, Seth? What'll be the next step?"

At that moment, he so desperately wanted to tell her how he truly felt about her. He wanted to take her in his arms and tell her how much he loved her. Instead he said, "The next step is for you to get some sleep, and then you, Maggie, and I'll figure out the next plan of action tomorrow. Okay?"

"Okay," she smiled, as she moved closer to Seth and hugged him closely. "Seth, I never did thank you."

"For what?"

"Seth," she said her eyes so heavy and tired, "I can't believe you've so easily forgotten. You saved my life." (*And*, she wanted to add but didn't, *for being there for me, for believing in me, for being the most wonderful man I've ever met . . .*)

Mel, locked up at the police station, was pacing in his holding cell like a caged animal. (*Damn it. How in the world could they've known what we were up to? Roger and I were so careful*, Mel thought as he quit pacing and lay down on the plastic foam mattress on the bunk.)

Initially, he and Roger had just done some drinking together. Renée had never been big on drinking, and when they had started dating, he had made a fresh resolve to completely quit himself. Looking back on his past and the trouble in which he had been involved, all of it had been a direct result of his drinking. So early in his and Renée's relationship, he had told her he didn't like alcohol. This was partly the truth; he didn't just like it. He loved it. Even in spite of all the problems it had caused him, he just couldn't seem to muster enough will power to stay away from it.

He had started his job as a cook at a small restaurant working from about four in the afternoon to nine at night with every other weekend off. Mel had considered it a job beneath him, but it was a way to temporarily bring money to the table. He was always in search of a way to make the big bucks without having to work too hard. Renée hadn't expected him to make a six figure income; she just had asked that he would be employed. He had been resentful at Renée for making him work at his dead-end job. But after buying the house and deciding to get engaged, he knew that he had to bring in money somehow. He knew deep down that without Renée in his life, he would have nothing, be nothing. So whenever she brought up the idea of leaving, he turned on the charm full blast and made promises upon promises until he had her right back where he wanted her. He would behave himself for awhile, and then he would eventually resume the lifestyle to which he had grown quite accustomed. Living his life how he wanted, looking out for number one, himself, and that was it.

Roger had been one of the short order cooks at the restaurant, and after smoking a few joints together, Mel had found out Roger's job was just a cover up. He had used his place of employment to establish a neutral area to promote his real means of making money which was selling drugs. For awhile, it had worked out perfectly. So many people had come in and out of the restaurant that no one had suspected that he had been providing a service other than preparing food for the customers.

"The business," as Roger had called it, had stared expanding. As a result, Roger's boss had begun to suspect that something had been going on. Before he could get fired, Roger quit. It wasn't too difficult to convince his clientele that a new location would be more beneficial for everyone. However, he had needed a business partner. So he had asked Mel. He didn't particularly like or trust him, but he had wanted someone who was ignorant enough to do his dirty work.

When Roger had proposed his role in his business, Mel had jumped at the idea of making easy money and getting out of his job as a cook. He thought he could get Renée off his back, and he could support his own growing habit of using. Although Renée was quite intelligent, she was extremely ignorant when it came to anything to do with drugs. (*She won't suspect a thing*, Mel had thought.) He had shaken Roger's hand, and they had become business associates.

Unfortunately, Mel didn't know he was getting involved in a drug ring that the Narcotics Division had been tracking for about three months. The business had grown significantly when Mel joined the team, not because he was especially good at what he did, but because he hadn't yet learned the tricks of the trade of negotiation. Put in simplest terms, Mel was doing the majority of the dropping off and picking up of packages. He was doing the dirty work, and Roger was reaping the benefits of collecting the money. Mel was given a cut of the profits, and enough drugs to pacify him. That in itself seemed to keep him coming back.

The little business had been doing well until Jake Benson became personally involved when his nephew had almost over-dosed from some bad drugs that were linked to Roger and Mel's operation. As a result, Benson had tripled his efforts to bring the drug ring down, and the extra efforts had finally paid off.

"You can't hold me in here! I have rights! I have at least one phone call! Let me call my dad!" Mel screamed from behind the bars of the holding cell.

"Would you just shut up?" an older policeman said as

he glared at Mel. "You'll get your damn phone call."

"Here's the list of charges," Jake said as he set the piece of paper on the lieutenant's desk. "This little jack-ass really got in over his head this time. Just look at what we have on him." Jake proceeded to read aloud the charges, "Possession of a controlled substance with intent to sell, resisting arrest, fleeing an officer, assaulting an officer, felon in possession of a fire arm, not to mention the terroristic threats and the domestic abuse. The woman he was living with . . . he messed her up pretty good."

"She knows she'll have to testify when this goes to trial, right?" questioned the lieutenant.

"Yeah," Jake said looking back at Mel. "Yeah, she does. You know, it never ceases to amaze me how some women can get involved with men like him." He shook his head as he took the paper from the lieutenant and silently reread the list of charges. "It boggles my mind, but I see it happen more than I care to admit, successful, talented women falling for pathetic losers."

"You think she knew about the drug ring?"

"No, no. I'm sure she didn't. She just got messed up with the wrong guy."

An hour later, Adam, Mel's dad arrived at the station. Because the lieutenant was a friend, he had agreed that Adam could briefly talk with Mel. He sat across from Mel in a small room. The large table separated the two, and to the back of them was a large two-way mirror. "So," his dad said, folding his hands in front of him on the table, "it looks like you really got yourself into a mess this time." He leaned back in his chair and adjusted his glasses. He ran his hand through his short, salt and pepper hair, sighed, and looked directly into the eyes of his son.

"Pop," Mel said as he rocked back on his chair, "I was set up. There has to be something you can do. Come on, you can get me a good lawyer, right?"

His dad remained silent for a few minutes, and then carefully chose his words. From past experiences, Adam knew how easily Mel could lose his temper, even if it was over a seemingly trivial matter, and this matter was anything but trivial. Adam had read the police report, and he knew deep within him that his son had gotten himself into something out of which he could not even get him out. Driving to the police station, Adam had been angry. "Why," he had said over and over to himself, "would Mel get himself mixed up in something like this? And to treat Renée like he had." He thought of Renée. The poor girl had been through a lot. Deep down, Adam regrettably felt some responsibility for it. He had wanted Renée and Mel's relationship to work out so badly, that he would have done anything to ensure that the couple would stay together. A while back, he had sensed some uncertainty coming from Renée, so at his suggestion, the two of them had lunch. Adam had felt the luncheon had been advantageous, from his viewpoint anyway. Renée had agreed that perhaps she was not giving Mel the benefit of the doubt, and that she wanted to give their relationship another chance. That was when Adam had brought up the idea of buying the house. He had told her that some friends of the family were selling it, and maybe it would be just what Mel and Renée needed, a place of their own. Renée was skeptical about their financial situation, but Adam had assured her that he would do anything he could to help them out. He broke away from his thoughts, and answered his son, "Mel, I'll do what I can, but there's a lot of evidence against you."

"Screw that!" Mel sputtered as he quickly stood up, knocking over his chair. "What? What're you trying to tell me, Pop, that you don't believe me either?"

"I didn't say that, Mel," Adam said. "What I'm trying to say is that I'm really concerned about what's going to happen to you."

Just as Adam was finishing trying to reason things out

with his son, the lieutenant swung open the door and said, "All right, that's about enough." He turned towards Adam. "Time for you to leave."

Adam stood up, gave Mel one last look and said, "Let me know if there's anything I can do."

"Yeah," Mel said glaring at the lieutenant, "get me out of this damned hellhole and away from these pigs."

Adam's entire body tensed as he walked by the lieutenant. He heard the lieutenant comment to Mel as he left the room, "You're one sorry excuse for a son."

Adam left the police station, got in his black BMW, took out his cell phone, and dialed Renée's number. She was his last chance. If only he could somehow persuade her to drop the charges against Mel, maybe the other charges could be lessened as well. The thought of Mel sitting all alone in that cell saddened him deeply. Although he knew that Mel had gotten himself into this mess, Adam was going to do everything in his power to get him out. He just hoped that all his colleagues at the hospital would not learn of his son's latest escapade. It was difficult to maintain a certain degree of professionalism when his son was continually in and out of trouble. The past year and a half, when Mel and Renée had been together, had truly been a blessing. He had felt, at last, that his obligation to try and keep Mel from making poor decisions had been lifted. With Renée in Mel's life, he had felt like Mel may be on the right track by finally finding what was missing to fulfill his life and make him happy. That was until last night. He did not know what had snapped in Mel, but he had seen it happen before. He had just hoped- oh, how he had hoped- and prayed that this time things would have been different. Unfortunately, they seemed to be taking the same direction as they had in the past.

"Hello?" Renée answered. When she read the number on the caller ID, her first instinct was not to take the call.

But her curiosity had gotten the best of her wondering what in the world Adam could want.

"Renée," resounded Adam's concerned voice over the phone. He nervously continued, "Ah . . . this is Adam. Renée, I'm so sorry. I was wondering how you were doing."

"Well," Renée said, "I've been better. I imagine you heard what happened."

"Yes, yes, I just came from the police station." He paused momentarily and then continued, "Renée, Mel's so sorry. He feels so terrible about everything that happened. Uh, is there anything I can do to help? Anything at all? Do you need any money or anything?"

(*Yeah, just throw money at the situation, and it's bound to get better.*) That had always been Adam's answer. Whenever she and Mel had an argument, usually about money, or when Mel did something to upset her, there was Adam, checkbook in hand, asking, 'How much will you need?' (*Not this time*, thought Renée as she silently promised herself that she was going to remain strong.) This time she was going to stand up for herself. She was not going to let Adam manipulate her in the way she had allowed in the past. Like with Mel, she had so wanted to believe all the words Adam had spoken to her. She had wanted to believe that she and Mel were going to work through things, and that everything was going to be all right. But she had recently realized it never was. As much as she had prayed and believed that someday things would change, she knew deep down in her heart that they never would. "No," Renée said with very little emotion, "I really don't need anything at this time."

"Oh," Adam said. There was an uncomfortable pause. Adam finally broke the silence by saying, "Renée, I would really like to get together with you and, well, talk about your future. And maybe talk about your future with Mel."

Renée took the phone away from her ear and blankly

stared at it. It took everything in her not to hang up. She could hardly believe that after everything that had happened, Adam would suggest that she and Mel had a future together. She finally lifted the phone to her ear and said, "Well, to be truthful, Adam, I'm going to need some time. I'm not in any condition to make any long term decisions at this point. Right now, I'm basically taking one thing at a time."

"Of course, of course," Adam stated, and Renée could hear the nervousness in his voice. "But when you're ready, Renée, please give me a call . . . or would you like me to call you?"

"We'll be in touch," Renée replied tiredly and proceeded to hang up the phone. The last thing she wanted to do at that moment, or at any time ever, was to continue that conversation. It was her hope that Adam would come to accept the fact that she and Mel were over, for good.

Renée thought of how much Adam had enabled Mel throughout their relationship. She wondered how she could have been so naïve as to what was going on. Mel was a master manipulator, but Adam had also been extremely convincing as to why he believed Renée should stay with Mel. Whenever Renée said it was over and she was leaving Mel, Adam had been there assuring her that Mel would change and that things would be different. It was not that Adam was a bad man, Renée concluded. As bizarre as it sounded, it seemed that he did not want to be responsible for Mel anymore, so he made Renée feel like she should be. Like if she loved him, she should be willing to pick up the pieces and always began anew. It was as if she was expected to continue to go forward like nothing had ever happened, and things were going to be okay. (*It must've been a great relief for Adam to turn over the obligation of taking care of Mel to me.*). Of course, she knew she had no right to be too bitter toward him. He did not force her into anything. Maybe forcing was too strong of a word . . . influenced would be a more accurate term, Renée conclusively decided.

"Who was that?" Seth asked in a concerned but nonchalant way. He saw the sad, disgusted look on Renée's face. He stood in the doorway of the living room waiting for her answer.

"Mel's dad," Renée said looking up at Seth. "He wanted to talk about my future, but not just my future . . .," she took a deep breath, "more accurately, my future with Mel."

"Oh," Seth said his eyes widening. He walked in the room, gestured to the spot beside Renée on the couch, and asked, "Want some company?"

Renée acceptingly nodded, and Seth sat down. "I just don't get it, Seth. His dad," she gave Seth a disgusted look, "I mean, I know he's his dad, but shouldn't there be a point where a parent draws the line?"

"Not in all cases, Renée." Seth continued, "You know, I've know Mel for quite a few years. For as long as I've know him, whenever he's been in trouble, he's looked to his dad to bail him out."

"But why," Renée questioned, "does Adam keep doing it? Wouldn't there come a time that he would give up and let Mel stand on his own two feet?"

Seth shrugged his shoulders. "Unfortunately, there're a lot of parents that place their success or worth in life on the success of their children. If their kids succeed, then they've succeeded as well. If their kids don't, then they feel as if they've failed too."

"I guess that makes sense. But don't you think that if Mel's dad wouldn't keep bailing him out and let him face some of his consequences, that it'd do him some good?"

"You're probably right, Renée, but that just isn't how Adam operates."

"You know," Renée said in reflection, "I feel used by Adam, too. I feel like he told me what I wanted to hear, helped us out financially, and helped us get into this house, so he wouldn't have to take care of Mel anymore. It was like as long as I was there, he didn't have to worry about him. But, on the other hand, I can't blame him for the mess I'm in. The truth is I made the decision to stay with him."

"Renée," Seth said in a comforting voice, "that may be true, but there's a lot to be said for the power of manipulation. Don't be too hard on yourself."

Renée sat quietly for a while, and then she turned to Seth and asked, "Would you like to know how he asked me to marry him?" Without waiting for Seth's reply, she continued, "He asked me sitting at the dining room table," she lifted her arm and despondently pointed. "Over there. His dad had stopped by to visit, and Mel said, 'Hey, Pop, I have something really important to ask Renée. Come and sit down with us.' We sat at the table, and I tell you, I had no idea what in the world he was going to ask. He got down on one knee, and he pulled out this ring." She took the ring off her finger and looked at it with disgust. Then she threw it across the room. Renée shook her head, and then said with a tear running down her face, "What a bunch of crap! I never meant anything to him! I feel like such an idiot!"

"Hey, hey," Seth looked into her eyes. "Renée, how could you've known? The important thing is that you *are* getting yourself out. What if you would've gone through with the wedding? You were blinded by the belief that he was going to change, and there were times that you really believed he had." He took a deep breath and honestly continued, "It's not going to be easy, but you *will* make it through this." He gently brushed away a tear that was falling down her cheek. He felt awful. Never in his life had he been so angry for being right. His hunch about Mel selling drugs had been confirmed, and he wondered if he should have told her earlier. (*Would it have mattered? Probably not. Would she have believed me? I'm not sure.*) "You know things are going to be okay, don't you?"

Renée took a deep breath, looked earnestly into Seth's eyes, and answered, "Yes. It just hurts." She rested her head on her knees that were pulled into her chest. After a moment she turned her head to the side, so she could look at Seth and asked, "Just tell me one thing, Seth, when *does* it get better?"

Seth knowingly replied, "In time, honey. In time."

# Chapter X

A resolve Renée had been contemplating for a while became final. The next week there was a "For Sale" sign in her yard. Although it was a decision she had made with confidence, it had still been an emotional one. She, Maggie, and Seth had met with various real estate agents, and they had finally all agreed on a middle-aged gentleman who seemed genuinely to have Renée's best interest at heart. The three of them had sorted through Renée's and Mel's possessions. Mel was still being held without bond in jail, and Renée, upon the selling of her house, found a one bedroom apartment into which she could move immediately. She had honestly told the landlady about her situation, and the kind, middle-aged woman had promised to help Renée anyway she could to make the transition go as smoothly as possible. Fortunately, the market was exceptionally good, and it was her hope and prayer that the house would be sold as soon as possible.

When Renée had started looking for an apartment, there were many that would not allow pets. This had saddened

Renée, as her dog, Tyon, had been a part of her life for the past five years. There was no way that she was about to give him away so landlords would look more favorably on her as a tenant. She had kept searching. Finally when she thought there would be nowhere she really wanted to live that would take pets, she had found the perfect apartment. It was a one bedroom, but it had a wide-open floor plan that was to Renée's satisfaction. The walls had just been painted, and the carpets had been newly shampooed. It was impeccably clean with new appliances, and most importantly, the landlady had agreed that for an additional deposit, Tyon could also live there.

Tears of happiness had streamed down Renee's face as Linda, the landlady, had confidentially told her, "Well, the policy is that we really aren't supposed to have dogs in the building. But honey," she had continued with a genuine, understanding smile, "I think you've been through enough. Let's just let it go. Okay?"

It had taken everything in Renée not to grab Linda and hug her to show her immense gratitude. Renée knew she had bent the rules for her and was extremely humbled at how God truly works in mysterious ways.

It eased Renée's fears when, within the first few days, there were several people who had made appointments with the realtor to view the house. Renée had made it very clear that her intent was not to make a profit, but to sell the house as quickly as possible. To her delight and surprise, by the end of the week, she had signed a Purchase Agreement. Due to Mel's poor credit score, it had not been advantageous to have him on the loan for the mortgage. Therefore, his name had not been put on the title either. Renée was the sole owner, and thus was in charge of selling it. (*Interesting*, Renée thought as she brought the last of Mel's boxes to the garage where she and Adam had made arrangements for him to pick up Mel's things, *Mel had always told me things like 'Good luck selling your house' or 'You'll never sell this house with me living in it.*') When she recalled these negative memories, she knew without any question that this truly had been the right decision. She also knew beyond a shadow of a doubt that there was no turning back now.

Exhausted from cleaning, moving boxes, and barely sleeping for the past couple of nights, Renée sat in the empty dining room, leaned her head against the wall, and started to cry. She thought of all the dreams she had had for their home together. "Why," she asked aloud in the silence, "couldn't things have worked out?" She thought back to the first days she and Mel had been dating. He had been so sweet, so charming, and now she felt it had all been a lie. It had just been a way to manipulate her into believing that he was this wonderful man, the answer to her prayers. She thought back to when they had purchased their home. The two of them had been like children. They had talked endlessly about their future starting with their wedding, raising a family, and all the memories they would share together in their new house. (*All a lie. And I was dumb enough to believe all of it.*) She closed her eyes, but the tears continued to fall.

* * *

Right from the start, Renée had been uncertain about the purchasing of the house. But Mel had convinced her to at least take a look at it. So on a Sunday afternoon, she, Mel, and his dad, who had set up a showing with the realtor, had driven to the house.

"Well, what do you think?" Mel had questioned excitedly walking from room to room.

"Well," Renée had answered honestly, "it's going to need some work . . ."

"It definitely has character," Adam had butted in and did not allow Renée to finish her sentence.

"Yes, it does," Renée had begun until she was again

rudely interrupted.

"I think it's perfect," Mel had decided. "We're going to take it."

"Maybe we should talk about this," Renée had interjected.

"Oh, come on, Renée," Mel pleaded, "where we gonna find a place like this at such a good price?"

"Well, the price might be lower because of all the work it needs," Renée had shot back a little too defensively, as Adam had given her a look of disappointment.

"Listen, Renée," Adam had said with a smile, "this seems like a wonderful opportunity for the two of you. As I had told you, I know the people who're selling the house. I'm sure they'll even cut you a better deal. If there's anything that the two of you need, well, all you have to do is ask. Perhaps I could arrange it so I could pay the closing costs, so you won't have to worry about that. It would be my house warming present. What do you think?"

* * *

"Looks pretty empty."

Renée eyes flew open, feeling as if her heart was going to beat out of her chest. "Seth," she said from her spot on the floor, "I didn't even hear you come in. You scared the crap out of me."

"Sorry," he said looking down at her. "I just stopped by to see if you needed anymore help and to drop this off." He held a key in front of her.

"I was wondering how you got in," Renée told him as she uncrossed her legs and got up from her spot on the floor. Taking the key she added, "I forgot that you and Maggie still had your keys."

"Well, I figured I could camp out on the floor until. . ." Seth tired to make light of the situation, but then stopped and took a more serious look at Renée. Seeing the tears dried on her face, he carefully changed the direction of what he was saying. "Oh, Renée, hey, I was only kidding. You know that I've a place to stay until my apartment is ready. I'm sorry. I shouldn't have . . ." he trailed off as Renée remained quiet. Not really knowing what to say he added, "Maggie is staying with Joe, and . . ."

"Seth, I'm really going to miss the two of you. Do you know that?" She continued sadly, not waiting for him to comment, "It may sound odd but the past couple of months, having you and Maggie staying here, were some of the happiest times I've had in a long time. You'd think that living here with my fiancé would've made things wonderful, but no. No, no matter how much time I spent painting, decorating, and rearranging things, this house never felt like a home until the two of you moved in. And now," she took a deep breath, "I get to move from this two-story house into a one bedroom apartment. The weird thing about it is that that isn't what's bothering me. What's really bothering me is that I won't get to see you and Maggie every day."

Although tears began sliding down her cheeks, Renée started laughing in spite of herself. She was thinking back to one of the many comical times she, Maggie, and Seth had together. "Remember the time we sat around the table and tired to see who could stuff the most marshmallows in their face?"

"Yeah," Seth laughed and rolled his eyes, "how could I forget that?

It was a rainy Saturday. We had planned on going to a matinee, but Maggie had persuaded us that playing with marshmallows was going to be so much more fun."

Renée continued laughing and questioned, "How does she come up with this stuff? That girl really does beat to her own drum, doesn't she?"

"No," Seth stated in obvious disagreement with Renée, "it is *not* her own drum. It's more like her own entire band."

\* \* \*

Seth, Maggie, and Renée had initially been discussing whether they should go to a movie or the mall. Seth had said no way to the mall idea, so they had been looking through the newspaper to find what movies would be playing that afternoon Maggie, who had not been completely interested in seeing a show, had told them of a fabulous game. The point of it was to see how many marshmallows they could stuff in their mouths at a time while repeating a phrase. (A phrase now, Renée, for the life of her, could not remember.) Because of Maggie's persistency, the three of them had found themselves sitting around the table in the dining room laughing so hard that tears had been pouring down their cheeks. Their fun abruptly had come to an end when Mel came home and had demanded to know what the hell was going on.

\* \* \*

"Renée," Seth began, causing Renée to let go of the memory and focus on the present, "it's not like we're disappearing from your life or something. You'll still get to see us." (*Because I need to see you, Renée*, Seth wanted to add but didn't.) "Uh, Renée, do you think that sometime. . ." Before Seth could finish his sentence, his cell phone rang. He looked at the number, disappointedly turned to Renée and said, "I'm sorry. I have to take this call."

Renée nodded. As she started walking towards the kitchen, she heard Maggie's voice from the driveway. "Renée! Renée!" Maggie almost knocked Renée over as she came running through the door. "Did the realtor get a hold of you? Well, good news there, dear, your house is as good as sold. You have a closing date next week!"

"Oh, what a relief," sighed Renée as she felt, for the first time in a long time, that she was able to relax and breathe a little more easily. "That's very good news. Now I can tell Linda that I can move into the apartment."

Maggie excitedly wrapped her arm around Renée's shoulder in a half hug. "I think I'm more excited than you are!" Renée just laughed. Before she had a chance to comment, Maggie looked around and asked, "Where's Seth? I saw his car parked in the driveway."

"Phone call. He said he *had* to take it." Maggie gave Renée an odd look. Although she didn't say anything, her body language questioned *what's that all about?* Renee just shrugged her shoulders.

"Wow," Maggie commented looking around the house, "this is way empty. You really got rid of a lot of stuff."

"Yeah, "Renée said, "Mel's things are packed in the garage. I put them there until his dad could come and pick them up. The necessities I need are in storage or in my car, and the rest I donated. I didn't need all that clutter in my life right now anyway."

"Good idea," Maggie said shaking her head in agreement. "As odd as it sounds, it'll probably be really cleansing to get rid of a lot of those memories."

"I think so too." Renée smiled and then, although she tried to stop them, tears began falling down her face.

"It'll be okay, Renée. It will, I promise," Maggie said as she hugged Renée tightly. "I know this is all happening so quickly, but it *is* the right thing. You know this, right?"

"Yes," Renée whispered. She impatiently brushed the tears away. "I'm just so sick of crying. Can you tell me when that will stop?"

"In time," Maggie knowingly replied. "In time."

Renée and Maggie sat on the floor and talked quietly amongst themselves as they waited for Seth to get off the phone.

"So," Maggie said propping herself up with her elbow, how did your meeting go the other day with Mel's dad? I bet that was a ton of fun."

"Yeah, a lot of fun..."

* * *

Out of an obligation, uncertainty, fear, or just because it was what she had felt was the right thing to do, Renée had agreed to meet with Adam at a small Italian restaurant for lunch. She had been seated at a small table, facing the widow, when she had seen him walk up the sidewalk. The lines in his face were creased with sadness. His gait was slower than usual, and Renée could see what a toll the past weeks events had taken on him. For a moment, she had felt so guilty that she had wanted to rush from the table, hug him, and tell him that she and Mel would work things out, and that things would be okay. Fortunately, she had stayed seated and waited for the inevitable. She knew he would start with small talk, ask how she was, how things were going, and then he would invariably turn this focus to Mel. It was always about Mel. It saddened her to think that this intelligent, successful, moral, good-hearted man could not break free from the power that his son had over him.

"Hello, Renée," he had said politely with a slight smile. "Mind if I sit down?"

"Hello, Adam," she had gestured to the chair across from her. "Please, have a seat."

"Renée," he had said. His eyes which were still somewhat red from crying pleaded with her from behind his glasses, "I hope you know how truly sorry I am... I... just don't know what to say."

That morning, getting ready for lunch, Renée had done her best to disguise the bruises on her face with makeup. Although it had helped, she knew they were still quite visible. She had felt Adam's eyes looking at them as she had intently tried to study the menu. He had been at a loss for words. She had waited patiently for him to say what he had come to say. She was so tired of pretending that everything was okay.

"Renée, I don't know what your future plans are, but . . .," he had cleared his throat and had carefully searched for the right words. Words that he thought if spoken would make Renée want to stay with Mel and, give him one more chance; just the same as she had always done in the past. "I honestly need to know if there's any chance that you'll try and work things out with Mel. He truly does love you so much, Renée, and he's so sorry for what happened. The first thing he asked when I went to see him was if you were okay."

"Did you tell him the truth?" Renée had asked, surprised at the forwardness in her voice. "Did you tell him that I'm *not* okay? That I'm scared? That I feel like my whole world has been turned upside down? I trusted him, believed in him, loved him, and then he treated me like a useless piece of trash that he intended to discard. Adam, as difficult as this is for me to say, and as difficult as it is for you to hear, I *have* to move on. I can't- no, I won't- stay with Mel." She had tried hard to fight back the tears, but it was to no avail as they had begun sliding down her cheeks, smearing her makeup and revealing the bruises beneath. "I'm never going to let anyone treat me like this again, never. No one deserves this. I tried. I tried with all my heart. But you know what? I've come to the cold, hurtful realization that Mel doesn't care about anyone but himself. If I would stay with him, what kind of life would I have? Not knowing if he's going to come home and beat the crap out of me, threaten my life, or what about paying bills? Do you realize that I had to rent out rooms in our home to make money to help pay the mortgage because Mel wouldn't work?" Renée had stopped, took a deep breath, and without giving Adam a chance to comment, she had continued, "And we, well, maybe it was more me, had dreamed of starting a family after we were married. Could you imagine what kind of life our children would have? No, no," she had shaken her head in an attempt to emphasize the point and also stop the tears that would not stop falling, "I'm looking towards my future, but it's not with Mel. Nothing you or anyone else can say will change my mind. I know he's your son and you love him, but I can't be caught in this vicious cycle any longer. I can't. I won't. I'm sorry if you believe I'm being callous and insensitive, but it's over between us, for good. I don't know when Mel's going to be released from jail, but I've already gone ahead with plans for selling the house. If you'd like, I will store his things in the garage and you can pick them up. Everything will all be there. I won't wreck any of his things or take anything that doesn't belong to me."

Renée had stood up, ready to leave. She no longer had an appetite. Adam had gently reached for her arm, looked into her swollen, red eyes, tears dampening his own cheeks. "Renée," he had answered honestly, "I know you won't take his things. Never has a day gone by that I've questioned your honesty or integrity. I'm just so sorry. I truly am, and I'm going to miss you more than you know. You truly are a wonderful person, and yes, you do deserve to be happy. Perhaps it was selfish of me, but I always thought that you'd be happy with Mel. I was wrong." He had lightly let go of her arm and slowly stood up. To Renée's surprise, he had reached out his arms to hug her. Quietly he had said, "Good-bye, Renée. Even though you and Mel were never married, I'll always consider you my daughter-in-law. I truly mean that."

Renée was at a loss for words. She grabbed her purse and walked out of the restaurant. She knew, if she could help it, this would be the last time she would talk with him ever again. Although Adam was a very good man, he had a weakness that he would never overcome. The bond was too strong between him and his son, and Adam was never going to give up enabling him.

\* \* \*

Seth looked like he had seen a ghost. His face was white, and his cell phone hung loosely in his hand. He looked from Renée to Maggie and back to Renée again.

"Oh, my gosh, Seth? What the hell's wrong with you?" Maggie asked as she rose to her feet.

Renée still seated in a cross-legged position on the floor looked up at him and asked with care, "Seth? Seth? What happened?" When Seth didn't say anything nor move from his position, she slowly got up, stood in front of him, peered up into his eyes, and repeated, "Seth, what is it?"

Seth shook his head from side to side. He opened his mouth to speak, but nothing came out. Finally, after taking a deep breath, he shook his head again from side to side and said, "You're not going to believe this. . ."

"Well?" Maggie and Renée's question seemed to be in unison.

He looked down at the floor and almost soundlessly responded, "Kathy's pregnant."

Renée's eyes got big, and she covered her mouth with her hand. "Oh, Seth."

"Are you the father?" Maggie asked confusedly. "I don't mean to be a bitch, Seth, but wasn't she *seeing* other guys when you were together?"

"Maggie!" Renée could not believe the boldness of Maggie's question, even though she had silently hoped, prayed that Seth had been wondering the same thing. She looked at him. His broad shoulders hung low; he looked as if he had just been punched in the stomach. His usually carefree and expressive eyes were shut tightly. His mouth was set in a hard, straight line.

"She says I am," Seth doubtfully admitted as he opened his eyes to look at Maggie and Renée. "What do I do?"

"Well," Maggie commented, staring at her perfectly filed finger nails obviously annoyed with Kathy's bold presumption, "I would totally get a paternity test. If I were you, there would be no way that that two-bit. . ."

"Maggie," Renée raised an eyebrow and shot her a sharp look. "Maybe Seth really doesn't need to hear that right now. Come on, Seth; Maggie and I are going to buy you a cup of coffee so the three of us can sit down and talk. I would offer you some here, but, well, just look around."

Seth looked at Renée with relief on his face and said, "Okay."

Maggie, Renée, and Seth sat at a small table at the coffee house. The place was somewhat run down and considered by many to be a dive. However, the three of them believed it had character. Thus, it had become a favorable place for them to frequent, a place where they could vent and unwind.

Looking across the table at Seth, Renée believed that that was just what Seth needed. "So, Seth, now what?"

"I guess I'm going to be a daddy," he replied softly, absently stirring his coffee.

"Like I said before," Maggie interjected, "I would find out for sure with a paternity test. Seth," she added clasping his hand in hers, "I know you probably think I sound heartless for saying this, but it seems kind of sudden that she would spring this on you. Don't you think? Really, Seth, it's obvious to her that you've moved on with your life, and she can't seem to accept the fact that she's no longer part of it."

Seth looked up into Maggie's eyes. The expression on his face pulled at Renee's heart strings. "I know. I know that what you're saying is true, but until I know for certain, I *have* to be there for the baby. Honestly, I could care less about Kathy, but if she's carrying my child. . ." He took a deep breath before continuing, "That baby is so innocent, and he *or she* deserves to have a father. You know? Growing up, I didn't have the best relationship with my dad. I promised myself a long time ago that when I became a parent, things would be different, a lot different. I just thought that I'd be in love with and married to the person who would have my baby."

Renée and Maggie exchanged a look of sympathy, and then Renée added, "Listen, Seth, no matter what, Mags and I'll be here for you. Okay? Whatever you need, just tell us."

"Thanks, thanks a lot," Seth said slouching in his chair with a look of worry mixed with uncertainty on his face.

He knew he didn't know a lot about babies, but he was willing to learn. He made a promise to this child that he would be there no matter what. No fear or uncertainty was going to allow him to waver on his decision. Although the terms on which he and Kathy split up were anything but friendly, he was willing to let go of any resentment he had towards her and put the welfare of his child first. He prayed that

Kathy would be willing to do the same.

# Chapter XI

A cool, still morning, Renée signed the papers and sold her house. Almost a month had passed since the horrific day when Mel had threatened her with a knife. Renée, feeling alone and vulnerable, brought the last of her things into the small, but cozy one bedroom apartment. Maggie and Seth had helped her move the majority of her things, but the remaining boxes she wanted to sort through herself. So after giving each of them a key, just in case something would happen, she hugged each of them tightly and watched them walk out the door.

When the afternoon arrived, the sun peeked through the numerous windows throughout her new home, and for the first time in a long time, Renée felt like things were truly going to be okay. She sat at her dining room table, blankly staring at the boxes which contained the minimal possessions which she had decided to keep. (*Where do I begin?*) Observing a smaller box that had PERSONAL, EXTREMELY IMPORTANT in bold, black letters written in Maggie's handwriting, she smiled as she opened it. On top of the box was a framed picture of Maggie, Seth, and herself. She picked it up and grinned as she recalled the event from the photo. The three of them had been at one of their many outings, a baseball game. Seth had found out Renée's passion for baseball, and he had gotten tickets to watch a minor league team play. Renée had been ecstatic. Mel had never taken her much of anywhere, especially to a baseball game. Mel hated baseball and could never understand Renée's love for the game. He always referred to it as boring and a waste of time. Renée observed the smiling faces looking back at her. Maggie's hair, at the time of the picture, was streaked with pink, and a hint of sunburn was evident on her nose and cheeks. Seth's head was titled slightly to one side, almost resting on Renée's shoulder. His brown eyes twinkled with mischief. "You're so handsome," Renée said aloud in the stillness of her new home. Then she looked at herself in the photo. She looked happy, very happy, unafraid, and secure. Not wanting to put the picture down, but knowing she had a lot of work on which to get started, she begrudgingly set it on the dining room table. For some reason, having the picture out in the open where she could see it helped her not to feel so alone.

Tyon lay in the middle of the room, soaking up the sunshine. "Well," she said to him as he lifted his head and wagged his tail, "it looks like it's just the two of us again. Come here, boy." Tyon obediently came to Renée and jumped into her lap. "It'll be okay, Tyon. This place is not permanent. It's just going to be a place to rest until we decide where we really want to go, or what we really want to do. Okay?"

He looked up at her and seemed to smile.

She thought about Seth and their talks on *The Stoop*. She wondered where he was and if he was okay. She missed him so much and wished things could have turned out differently between them. But for right now, she understood this was how it had to be. Seth needed time to decide what he and Kathy were going to do. They had to do what would be best for the baby. All she could do was to wait patiently and pray for guidance.

Seth and Kathy were on their way to the clinic for a prenatal visit. They drove in silence, as Seth really didn't know what to say to this woman. Finally, he asked her, "So how far along do you think you are- four months or so?" He quickly glanced to see if she had any signs of showing, but it was difficult to tell. He wasn't sure, as he wasn't that used to being around pregnant women.

Kathy turned to him, rolled her eyes, and answered, "How am I supposed to know? Do you actually think I keep track of this? I missed my period for about three or four months or something like that. I just thought I was irregular. It happens you know." She defensively added, "What? Do you think I planned on this happening? Listen, Seth, I'm about as excited about this as you are."

"I didn't say I wasn't excited."

"You didn't have to. You haven't exactly been Mr. Perky lately. I can read between the lines. I'm not as dumb as you think I am, Seth."

"Kathy," Seth said, trying to maintain his composure, "the truth of the matter is is that I'm still pretty shocked. You and I haven't been together for some time, and then I get a phone call from you telling me that you're pregnant. How did you expect me to react? As I remember, our relationship didn't end on the best of terms."

"Oh, yeah. Whatever, Seth. You're just upset because now instead of getting to hang out with those sluts you're usually with, you're stuck with me!" Sobbing, she buried her face into her hands and did not look up until Seth had parked the car in the parking lot of the clinic. He was upset about Renée and Maggie being called sluts, but given the present circumstances, he really did not want to get into a fight over that comment.

He shut off the engine, turned to her, gently lifted her chin so he could look into her eyes, and said, "Kathy, this has all come as a really big surprise. I'm sorry if you've taken that to mean that I don't care because I do. I truly do." She looked down, and was about to speak when Seth continued, "Will you please look at me, Kathy?" She lifted her head and looked into Seth's understanding and honest eyes. "Look, given the obvious circumstances, this isn't going to be easy. Not easy for you or me, but this is a baby that we're talking about, a baby. We have to be in this together. Kathy, you have my word that I'll be with you every step of the way. You believe me, don't you?"

"Yes," she finally replied slightly jutting out her chin, pouting like a child. "Well, what about those other . . .," she looked at Seth, careful not to repeat what she had called them before, "*girls?*"

"Maggie and Renée. Incidentally, Kathy, you're never to call them sluts or any other derogatory names *again*." He sighed and said, "They're my friends, Kathy. The three of us have gone through some pretty hairy stuff this past month."

"Yeah," Kathy commented, "I heard. I think Renée set it all up to frame Mel. I've never liked her or trusted her anyway. I always thought Mel was a pretty decent guy."

(*Of course you did*, thought Seth as he slid back into his seat). He turned to Kathy and said, "Look, Kathy, either we're in this together or not. Not to point out the obvious, but you must want me to be around to help with the baby or you wouldn't have called. Kathy, I told you I'd be here for the baby, and I mean it." He waited for a moment and sincerely questioned, "Is that what you want?"

"You mean we're going to get back together?" Kathy looked at him with hope in her eyes.

He again took a deep breath and picked his words carefully. "Well, not exactly, Kathy. Kathy, we tried to make a go of a relationship together, remember? It just didn't work. What I'm saying is that we have to put our differences aside so we can, together, bring this baby into the world. Kathy, I know you're probably very scared, and I am too. But this isn't something that's going to go away today, tomorrow, in a year, or ever. We're going to be parents, Kathy. This is a human being that we're going to be responsible for. I'm willing to do whatever it takes to make sure our child has as happy a life as we're able to give."

"Oh," Kathy said obviously disappointed. "But, Seth, I've changed a lot, and I think you're going to see that. I'm sorry that I've been so up and down, but I've never been pregnant before. I just don't understand a lot that's going on with me. Seth, I know that things weren't perfect between us before, and I also know that I'm a lot to blame. I wasn't always honest with you, and I know I didn't always treat you the best I could. But believe me when I say this, Seth, things *will* be different this time. I promise. But please, please don't leave me. I just don't know what I'd do without you."

She looked so sincere, sounded so genuine, that Seth could not fight back the urge to comfort her. "Come here," he said holding out his arms. "Everything's going to be okay. We're going to do this together."

As he gently stroked her hair, Kathy smiled. She had him right where she wanted him.

\* \* \*

Seth thought back to when he had met Kathy. He had had a tough day at work, so he and his friend stopped off at a local bar to relax and play a game of foosball- Seth's favorite way to let off steam- and wind down.

Kathy, who had been their waitress, had taken their order. Seth had asked her to bring him a Coke. When she had teased him about not drinking, he had been quick to state that he had abused the privilege so much that it had been taken away. Although not exactly interpreting its meaning, she had laughed at his comment. Seth had liked the way she had smiled. She had playfully pushed her blonde hair away from her blue eyes, and he had noticed the dimples on her cheeks. He had been lonely, and although his gut had told him that she was going to be nothing but trouble, he had ignored it. Eventually, as the evening had progressed, he half-heartedly asked her for her number. She willingly had given it to him and had insisted that he call her: the sooner the better. His friend had been surprised, as he knew Seth didn't make a habit of picking up women at a bar. His friend had quickly relayed to him that he thought she was a ditz; a hot ditz, but still a ditz. Seth had never intended for the relationship to escalate. Every time he had tired to break up with her, she'd cry. He had seen good in her and had kept thinking that maybe, somehow, she was going to change. Unfortunately, that had never happened. The last straw had been when he had caught her in bed with one of his good friends. It had taken everything in him not to smash his friend's head in. But to his credit, he had not gone over the deep end. He had yelled at them, but he hadn't thrown anything, punched any walls, or hit anyone. He had had enough and called it quits. Before leaving the apartment in which he had found his friend (or whom he had thought was a friend) and her together, he had told her she could pack up all her stuff from their apartment and leave. He had been paying the rent and all the bills, so he was damned if he was going to be the one to find a new place to live. But as with so many other things, Kathy had ended up having plans of her own.

\* \* \*

"Everything will be just fine," Seth said letting go of Kathy. "Now let's go in for your appointment." Walking to the passenger side of the car, he opened her door and said with reassurance, "Things are going to be okay."

Kathy smiled a secretive little smile. (*Yes. Yes, they will, Seth. More than you even know.*)

# Chapter XII

Juggling work as Youth Director, taking some night classes to keep herself qualified for her job, teaching aerobic classes on the weekend, and trying to arrange her apartment, kept Renée quite busy for the next couple of weeks. Although she had heard from Maggie via cell phone on a daily basis, Seth was not as adamant about keeping in touch. Renée missed him. She missed him more than she cared to admit. At night, after taking Tyon for a long walk, she would relax on her couch holding a cup of tea in one hand and the picture of Seth, Maggie, and herself in the other. Looking back, she wondered how she could have been so blind. How could she have not realized that there was more to their relationship than just an extremely close friendship? Of course she had thought he was handsome; she had thought that from the first day when she had met him, but there was more, much more. He was everything for which she was looking, but she had been too blind to see it. "Too late now, right buddy?" she asked aloud, reaching down to scratch Tyon's ear. "But hey, at least I have you, right?" The little black and white dog wagged his tail and licked her finger. Renée looked at her watch. It was 7:00 PM; Maggie would be at her house in about fifteen minutes. Earlier in the day, Maggie had called her at work and announced that she would be over that night. She was bringing Chinese food, and it would be just a girls' night. Renée would rather have had some down time and spent the evening alone curled up on the couch with Tyon, but she missed Maggie. Deep down, she was grateful she had invited herself over.

"Nice, very nice," Maggie said walking in the door carrying an armful of red and white containers emitting the delicious odor of Chinese food. Renée could smell the aroma, and her stomach started to growl. With her crazy schedule at work, she had barely found time to eat all day. (*Not a good habit to form*, she concluded.) She was definitely feeling the effects of her unintelligent decision.

"Smells very good," Renée told Maggie as Maggie shut the door. "I'm hungry, let's eat!"

"Give me a minute, give me a minute." Maggie walked around from room to room. "I have to hand it to you, Renée, you did a nice job with this place. So," she questioned plopping herself down on the couch, "have you missed me?"

"You've no idea," Renée smiled as she dished up a plate and gave it to Maggie.

"That much, huh?" Maggie asked studying Renée for awhile and then proceeded, "Have you been eating?"

"Yes."

"Doesn't look like it. Renée, you look like crap."

"Uh, thanks," Renée responded as she threw a pillow from the couch at Maggie. "You're so gracious! You invite yourself to my home, deprive me from eating right away because you have to check everything out, and then you insult me! What's the world coming to?"

Renée and Maggie both began to laugh.

"Seriously," Maggie said between bites, "how're you doing?"

"Okay . . . well, I don't know . . . it's just. . ."she stood up and walked to the window. "I don't know. It's a lot of things. Things have moved so quickly, you know? I mean it's only been a couple months since, well, you know what happened. You were there. And yet in an odd way, sometimes it feels longer." She turned to Maggie who was sitting cross-legged on the couch devouring her food. "Does this make any sense?"

Maggie nodded her head, swallowed a bite, and replied, "Yes."

Renée came back to the couch and sat beside Maggie. "I've been seeing a psychotherapist you know."

"Yes, you had told me that. Anyway. . ."

"She said I have a traumatic emotional bond to Mel, and until I break that, I'll never be in a healthy relationship."

"Makes sense. What else does she have to say?"

"She agrees with me that things did move quickly, but not to be too quick to question them because things generally happen for a reason."

"That sounds about right," Maggie said as she licked her fingers and eyed Renée's uneaten wan ton. "Are you going to eat that?"

"No, go ahead," Renée said with a laugh. "I guess I'm still having a difficult time adjusting to everything."

"Well, no kidding." Maggie rolled her eyes. "Renée, not to point out the obvious, but you've been through a lot the past couple of months. You know? You get the crap beat out of you by the loser you were engaged to, you have to get rid of most of your possessions, sell your house, move, kick your friends out of your house," she smiled. "Cut yourself some slack. It's going to take you some time to adjust." Maggie hesitated, but finally asked the question that was on her mind, "Ah, Renée, I was wondering if you'd heard anything about when Mel's trial is going to be? He's still being held without bail, right?"

"Yes, yes, he is. Thank God. I've spoken with Jake Benson, the one from the Narcotics Division, and he said it should be only a matter of days. He said that I helped the case a lot with all the information I gave him, which, honestly, I didn't think was that useful. Another thing I worry about is what happens if he does get released? Maggie, I know Mel, and he'll try to get back at me. Right now, I feel pretty secure and safe knowing he's locked up, but what if. . ."

"Renée, he's *not* going to be getting out any time soon. And," she smiled flexing her thin arm using the other one to push up the muscle trying to make it look larger than it was, "if he tries anything, he'll have to go through me first."

"Ha!" Renée laughed. "That really makes me feel secure and safe, Maggie. You're so big and tough!"

"Oh, shut up! I totally have been working out. Can't you tell?"

"No."

"Oh, whatever," Maggie said, rolling her eyes, trying to look extremely upset, but not succeeding.

Renée moved the food on her plate around with her fork. She looked up at Maggie and asked, "So, have you heard from Seth lately?"

"Uh, uh," Maggie said looking up at Renée from the floor. She had her feet up on the couch with her hands on her stomach. "I ate way too much."

"Nothing?" Renée inquired.

"Why?" Maggie asked, "Is there something you need to tell me?"

"What's *that* supposed to mean?" Renée asked slightly blushing. She hurriedly got to her feet and brought the dishes to the sink in the kitchen before Maggie could read what was so obviously written all over her face.

"Renée," Maggie leaned over and grabbed for her leg as she was going towards the kitchen but missed. "Renée, would you mind telling me what's going on?"

Renée kept her back to Renée, spraying the dishes off in the sink. When she felt the color finally dissipate from her face, she turned and said, "I don't know what you're talking about."

"Renée," began Maggie as she walked towards her, "you haven't been eating. It's obvious you haven't been sleeping, and you've been so easily distracted lately . . . oh, my gosh!" Maggie brought her hands to her cheeks, started smiling, and continued, "I can't believe I didn't put this together sooner."

"What?" Renée asked a little annoyed at this time with Maggie's drama queen antics.

"It's Seth," she continued smiling with assurance. "Yup." She drummed her fingers on her head like she was thinking. "Why did it take me so long to figure this out? Well, duh, now that I know, it's as obvious as the nose on my face!"

"Maggie," Renée asked giving her a blank look, "what're you talking about?"

"Renée, please! Don't insult my intelligence any longer. I still can't believe that I missed this one!"

"Okay, Maggie, this is really starting to get on my nerves. Spit it out."

To Renée's surprise, Maggie threw her arms around her in a large embrace and whispered in her ear, "You, dear Renée, are in love with Seth."

"Whatever," Renée said removing Maggie's arms from around her neck. "Don't be ridiculous. Seth and I are, and always have been, just friends."

"You're not fooling anyone, especially me." Maggie smiled and wagged a finger at Renée.

Renée took a deep breath, sat on the couch, and watched as Maggie leapt over the back of it and sat right next to her. "So," Maggie implored, "tell me! Tell me! When did this all start?"

"Maggie, for gosh sakes, you're acting like we're in junior high or something. There's nothing going on."

"Oh, I don't doubt for a minute that what you're saying is true. I know there's nothing going on, because I know you and I know Seth, and . . ."

"What?"

"First, you have to quit playing this game. I know you know I know, so cut the crap. Okay?"

Renée looked at Maggie and conceded by finally admitting, "Okay."

"Okay, first I want to know when this all started."

"I don't know, exactly," Renée said standing up. She began pacing. It was a nervous habit, and Maggie was definitely making her nervous. "I guess just over time, and I don't know that I'm in *love* with him. That's such a strong word." She sat down again next to Maggie. She pleadingly looked into her eyes and asked, "Maggie, what should I do? He and I have been through so much together. Maybe I'm just jumping to conclusions. Maybe what I'm feeling is a kind of hero worship or something."

"Uh, wrong answer, thanks for playing. Come on, Renée. There's always been a certain kind of chemistry between the two of you, and don't even say you deny it." Renée knowingly shook her head in agreement. "And, Renée, the reason why I said I know there's nothing going on between the two of you is because neither of you would feel it's the right time. I mean holy crap. Not to point out the obvious, but Seth is in a real tough spot right now. He doesn't love Kathy- that's so evident- but he wants to do the right thing by the baby. And you know this too, so you respect that."

"Yeah," Renée said knowing that Maggie was unequivocally correct. "But, Maggie, how do you know that Seth even feels the same way I do?"

"Renée, I'm not the greatest person in the world to make any speculations about love or relationships in general, but Renée, I've seen the way Seth looks at you when he doesn't think you're looking. I've seen this macho, tough guy literally melt when you walk into the room. Honestly, I've known Seth for a long time, and I've never seen him act this way around any other woman."

"Has Seth ever said anything to you?"

"He didn't have to, Renée. I could read it all over his face. Honestly, I just thought he would get over it, because I didn't think there was a chance in hell that you'd reciprocate the feelings. I didn't want to see him get hurt. God, Renée, you were so caught up in Mel that if Seth would've said anything to you, would you've possibly believed him?"

"No, probably not," Renée admitted. "I probably would've thought he was just feeling sorry for me or something."

"So, what're you going to do now?"

"What do you mean?" Renée gave her a confused look. There's nothing I really can do. You said it yourself, Maggie, he's with Kathy."

"Oh, no, no, no," Maggie sternly corrected her, "that is *not* what I said at all. What I said is that Seth's going to do the right thing by the baby. That doesn't mean he's getting or ever will get back together with Kathy."

"How can you be so sure, Maggie? A baby changes people's lives forever."

"Yes, I totally agree with you. They do. But when Seth and Kathy broke up, Seth made a decision that it was over between them, done, end of discussion. Seth's a strong person, Renée, and he's not one to go back on a decision as important as that one. Seth's no dummy. He knows what Kathy's like. You have my word; he's not going to get involved with her in that capacity again. Kathy hurt Seth really bad. He trusted her, and she crapped all over him. It hurt me to see him go through it, and it took everything in me not to say *I told you so*. Seth has a good heart, a lot like you, and he looks for the good in people. Did you know that he caught her in bed with one of his good friends?"

Renée eyes got wide with a look of surprise. "Wow."

You didn't know that, did you? You don't know Kathy that well, and you're lucky." Maggie shot Renée a knowing look and added, "She's one shallow, dishonest, self-centered piece of work."

"Oh," Renée said, surprised. "Seth never really said much about her except that things just didn't work out between them."

"That's Seth for you. He's not going to talk smack about someone just to make him look better. You know that saying *if you don't have anything nice to say, don't say nothing at all?*" Renée smiled. "Well, Renée, Seth pretty much lives by that. He's honestly one of the most morally decent, honest men I've ever met. But you know this, Renée. And I'm not going to tell you what to do, but I'm going to say this, you'd be a fool to not at least tell him how you feel."

"I don't know. I just don't know."

Maggie looked at her questionably. "What're you afraid of Renée? I'm a firm believer that in time the majority of people regret more of the things they didn't do in life than the things they did do. Right?"

Renée exhaled loudly and nodded.

Maggie continued, "Okay. Either one of two things is going to happen. One, you tell him, and- and I highly doubt this is going to happen- he explains to you that he is flattered, but that he doesn't feel the same about you. Or two, you tell him, and the two of you work through this together, and you have a wonderful relationship based on honesty, trust, and mutual respect. Hey, I'm no rocket scientist, but I'm pretty sure I know which decision I'd make if I were him. You know, Oprah once said on one of her shows,

'Knowing what you want to do with your life is the first step in making it happen.' You might want to think about that." Maggie watched Oprah religiously and was forever quoting her.

Renée resigned herself to the fact that there was a lot of truth in what Maggie had said. She had known for a long time that Seth was all of which Maggie had spoken and more; he was her best friend. But she didn't know if she was ready to take that step. "We'll see, Maggie. We'll see."

# Chapter XIII

Tuesday morning, on her way to work, Renée received a phone call from Jake Benson. He informed her that the trial date was set, and that she, Maggie, and Seth would have to testify. Because of the severity and the complexity of the charges and the distinct possibility that Mel could be a further menace to society, he was going to be held without bail at the local jail. Renée breathed a sigh of relief. The nightmares were not as frequent, but there were still many times that she had woken and could almost feel Mel's breath on her face, and hear the words that he had so emphatically whispered in her ear, "I'm gonna beat you like the dog you are and kill you like the dog you are."

Renée slightly shuddered as she pulled her car back into the mainstream of traffic from the shoulder of the road where she had been parked when talking to Jake. Since the first time Jake had spoken with her after being released from the hospital, Renée had had a good feeling about him. He was a little rough around the edges, brass and to the point, but she wouldn't exactly consider those character flaws. She believed he would do everything in his power to ensure that justice was served, including keeping Renée safe. That was why, she believed, the judge had denied the request to release Mel into the temporary custody of his dad until the trial. Normally, such a thing would have occurred, but fortunately for Renée, she had cooperated to the best of her ability with Jake, answering all his questions, and securing a lot of useful information for the prosecuting attorney.

Sadness swept over Renée as she continued driving. She tried to let it go, bringing to mind the horrific ordeal to which Mel had subjected her. But even in view of it, she still felt a pang of guilt knowing she would play a large part in convicting Mel, and she knew in her heart that he would be serving a substantial amount of time in prison. Firmly grasping the steering wheel, she shook attempting to shake herself free from the uneasy feelings and turn her attention to something that was even more pressing on her mind. "Seth," she smiled as she quietly spoke his name. As a young girl, she had never been one to believe much in fairy tales or knights in shining armor. But all he needed was the white horse, and her fantasy would be complete. She wondered how in the world she would broach the subject. How would she tell this wonderful, kind man how she truly felt? And would he be receptive to what she would tell him? If Kathy would not have gotten pregnant, things would not be so complicated, but the reality of the situation was that she had. Renée felt a pang of guilt as she thought of Kathy. (*What would I do if I was in her situation? Wouldn't I want the father of my child to be an integral part of my life too?*) Although Maggie had pled a good case, Renée could not help feeling that perhaps she was being selfish in the assumption that she should be so bold to tell Seth of her true feelings.

Just as she was pulling into the parking lot of the YMCA, Renée's cell phone began to ring. She looked at the caller I.D. and was excited yet nervous when she recognized the number. It was Seth. She cleared her throat and answered, "Hello."

"Renée, hi, it's Seth. I know you're on your way to work, but I need to talk to you."

She waited for him to continue. When he didn't, she offered, "Okay." Renée shifted her car into park, turned off the engine, and waited patiently for Seth to continue.

"Renée, there's a possibility that Mel is going to be released on bond."

"What?" Renée almost screamed into the phone. "That's impossible! I just spoke with Jake not too long ago, and he assured me that Mel wasn't going to be released."

"Well, his daddy seems to know some people, and he's been pulling a few strings. I just got off the phone with one my friends at the station, and he gave me the heads up as soon as he heard." He let out a breath and offered, "Renée, I know this scares you. If you want, I could stay over at your place."

"Seth," Renée said, brushing away tears of fear from her face, "I really don't think I need a watch dog to protect me."

Seth was quiet for a moment. "Renée," he continued sadly, "I didn't mean it like that. I just want to make sure that you're okay."

"I'll be fine," Renée said getting out of her car. "Listen, Seth, I have to go. I'm going to be late for work."

"Renée," he added quickly, "I know you're in a hurry, but I've one more important question." The uncertainty in Seth's voice surprised Renée. "Renée, do you have any idea why Kathy would go visit Mel? The same friend that told me about Mel's getting out on bail told me she had been there."

Renée's mouth hung open. She had no clue as to what to say, "Uh," she stammered. "Honestly, Seth, I've no idea."

"Neither do I," Seth let out a long sigh. "I guess I'm going to have to call her and find out. Just before he was to hang up he added, "If you need anything, anything at all, call me. Okay?"

"Okay." She hung up the phone and walked up the stairs of the YMCA building so she could go inside to work.

Seth sat in silence. He checked his watch. Was it too early to go to Kathy's apartment and confront her about going to see Mel? (*What in the hell was she doing?*) He shook his head. He had to think about work. Between taking Kathy to her prenatal visits and helping out Renée, he had already taken enough non-requested time off. Although his director was pretty lax, his last conversation had been one of suggesting that Seth take care of his personal business after hours. Even though the uncertainty as to why Kathy had been to visit Mel was gnawing at his insides, if he wanted to question her in person, he knew the matter would have to wait until his work day was over. Ever since their conversation in the car about the baby and Kathy's misunderstanding that they might get back together, she had begun calling him several times a day at the office. He had repeatedly asked her not to call unless it was of absolute necessity. For once, he was grateful she never listened. Maybe during one of those calls he could casually find out what in God's name she was up to.

As he was getting ready to leave, he grabbed his keys off the stand beside the door. He glanced down at the picture of Renée, Maggie, and himself. He picked it up and smiled. "How I miss you," he said aloud looking at Renée's face. He recalled the memory of the three of them going to the carnival, and what a time it had been.

\* \* \*

"Hey," Maggie had said, showing the flyer to Seth, "want to take the two hottest chicks in the neighborhood to the carnival?"

He had taken the flyer, looked up at Maggie, and in his most earnest voice had replied, "Yeah, as soon as you direct me to where they're hiding."

"You're such a jerk! I'm totally going to tell Renée what you said!"

"Tell me what?" Renée had questioned walking in the door. She had handed one bag of groceries to Seth and one to Maggie. "Here, help me put these away. Please?"

Maggie had looked at the bag, handed it to Seth, grabbed the flyer from the kitchen counter and showed it to Renée. "I asked Seth if he would take the hottest women in the neighborhood to the carnival, and he said that he would when he found out where they were hiding!"

"Tattle-tale!" Seth had accusingly commented. When Maggie had turned around, he had made a face behind her back.

Observing Seth's childish behavior, Renée had suppressed a giggle by putting her hand over her mouth. "Oh," she had said smiling at him, "funny, yes, very funny." Pretending to act like she was offended, she crossed her arms and had asked, "So, are you going to take us or what?"

* * *

Seth put down the picture, locked the door behind him, and headed out to his car parked in back. Since leaving Renée's house, he had moved into a one bedroom apartment, all he could find at the time. It wasn't in the best part of town, but it was a place to stay. He walked to his car and was shocked at what he saw. The driver's side tire was slashed, and the windshield, although still intact, had cracks spreading across it. "What the . . ." He cursed under his breath. He took out his cell phone and dialed his director's number. As he was waiting for Hal to pick up, he popped the truck, took out the spare, and started jacking up the car.

"Hello," echoed Hal's voice.

"Hal, it's Seth."

"Seth, don't even tell me you're not coming into work today. When we had our little discussion the other day, I thought I made it. . ."

"Listen," Seth said, cutting him off in mid-sentence, "I know what you said, but I've a slashed front tire and my windshield is cracked. I'm changing the tire as we speak."

"Holy, Seth, you've had quite the run of bad luck." He chuckled. "Not too much damage to Princess I hope."

Seth let out a frustrated groan. The first month on the job, still nervous, and trying to make polite conversation with his co-workers in the office, he had mistakenly told a guy about his car by telling him, "She's a beautifully restored 1969 Camaro, metallic blue with white interior, and I nicknamed her Princess." After the words had come out of this mouth, he instantly had wanted to take them back. Although not the most practical thing he owned, he had no intentions of selling her, ever. She was his baby. Everyone who knew him knew how much she meant to him. He had been skeptical about renting the apartment in this neighborhood because someone might do some damage to her. Unfortunately, he had been right to be leery.

"No, not too much damage. As soon as I get the tire changed, she'll be drivable at least. I'll be there as soon as I can. Okay?"

"Yeah, Seth," he stopped chuckling and seriously added, "but this'll be the last time."

"Yeah, okay. I'll be there as soon as I can." Seth hung up the phone and took a look around the car for any evidence pointing to whom the vandal could be. He had a horrible feeling in the pit of his stomach that he already knew who did it.

As he opened the door and was going to get into his car,

he saw a shiny object lying in front of the front tire. Walking around the open car door, he knelt down to pick it up. "Uh," he almost laughed, "a tube of lipstick." He was about to toss it away when something inside him prompted him to examine it a little more carefully. He unfolded his hand. Lightly carved on the lipstick case were the initials K.A.P. "No," Seth shook his head, "it can't be. . ." Seth hurriedly got into his car and got ready to drive to his office. He gave Kath's cell phone a call, but it went straight to voice message. "Damn," he said as he put down his phone. (*This is too much! First she visits Mel in jail, and now I find her lipstick tube lying by my banged up car.*)

Furious, he stepped on the accelerator. He was already late for work.

Walking into the office, one of his co-workers waved him over to his desk. "Say Seth, I didn't know it was customary to have personal visits at the office."

"What?" Seth asked confused as Aaron, his co-worker, grinned a self-righteous grin and jerked his thumb towards Seth's office. Inside sat Kathy. Her legs were crossed, revealing blank panties from below a too short skirt. She was wearing a loose top concealing her slightly expanding belly. Her blonde hair was tied back, and Seth wondered to himself if she had difficulty finding a shade of lipstick to match the color of shirt she was wearing.

"Oh, great," Seth grunted walking towards his office. He looked back at Aaron who was still smiling.

Seth stepped into his office and shut the door. He walked in front of Kathy, leaned against his desk, and crossed his arms in front of him. "Funny thing, Kathy, I was just trying to get a hold of you."

"Oh," she replied innocently, and stood up to give Seth a hug. "Did you miss me?"

Seth glared at her. "Sit down, Kathy." He continued to stare at her in silence, and then finally said, "That's an interesting color of lipstick you have on. Is it new?"

"Oh, Seth," Kathy squealed and clapped her hands obviously delighted that he had noticed. "Do you like it?"

Seth didn't answer the question, but instead he handed Kathy the tube of lipstick that he had found in the parking lot by his car. He looked her square in the eyes and angrily stated, "Not as much as this one."

Immediately, Kathy's smile faded. She shifted nervously in her chair.

Seth waited patiently for her to say something. When she didn't, he slammed his hand on his desk and turned to her. His voice shaking with anger he demanded, "Tell me what the hell's going on!"

"Uh, what do you mean?" she asked as innocently as possible.

"Cut the crap, Kathy. I found this lipstick by my car this morning. My car that had a slashed tire and the windshield cracked. So, I'm going to ask you one more time, what the hell's going on?"

Kathy started to cry. "Seth, oh, Seth! I just didn't want you to be mad at me! I. . . I. . ." she tried to regain her composure. "Seth, I'm going to get an abortion."

"What?" Seth asked his jaw dropping. "What did you just say? You're what?"

"I don't want this baby, and the baby's dad convinced me that you wouldn't want it either, so I was upset. I know you love that stupid car more than me, so when he suggested that we mess it up a little. . ." She sobbed into her tissue and then sorrowfully continued, "I never thought he would take it that far."

Seth almost fell over. He couldn't fully grasp what Kathy was saying. Then, as if a light bulb came on, he saw everything with the utmost of clarity. Now it all made perfect sense. He no longer had to ask Kathy why she was at the jail visiting Mel; he already knew the answer. He couldn't breathe. He felt like he was suffocating. He tried to speak, but no sound came from his lips. He stared at her. His mouth hung open in disbelief as he shook his head from side to side in complete bewilderment. He wanted to grab her, slam her into the wall, and scream. Instead, he struggled hard to regain his composure. When he finally did, he turned weakly to her and stated in a disgusted, grave voice, "Kathy, I suggest you leave right now."

"But, Seth, I was going to tell you about . . . about everything."

"When?" Seth gasped for air. "When the baby was five? What kind of sick demented joke is this, Kathy? What the hell were you thinking?" (*No wonder she couldn't figure out how far a long she was. No wonder she didn't want me in the room when the ultrasound was being conducted. And the baby. Oh, my God, this baby isn't mine . . . First I lose the chance to tell Renée how I truly feel about her, and now I lose this baby.*)

"Well," Kathy glared at him as she uncrossed and recrossed her legs, folding her arms in front of her, "you don't have to get so hostile on me. I thought Mel was going to be sent to prison, so what could I do? But after talking everything over with him when he got out on bail early this morning, he assured me that he's going to get out of the charges. So thanks, Seth, for all your help with taking me to my appointments and being there for me, but I don't need you anymore. Mel and I've talked it over. When we start our future together, we both agree that there's not going to be room for a baby in it. That's why I made the decision to have an abortion. I needed to let you know because I knew you would keep calling to check up on me." Kathy said all this so matter-of-fact that Seth could not believe what he was hearing.

She had come to his office and told him that he wasn't the father; that Mel was. And had he misunderstood, or did she tell him that she and Mel were planning a future together? He felt again as if his breath had literally been knocked out of him. He looked at Kathy with disbelief that she could be so calm about everything. He was completely at a loss for words.

Then a horrible realization came over him. Fear pulsed through his veins, and he could feel the sweat beads beginning to roll down his back. Suddenly, confronting Kathy about the car had lost its significance; it was no longer his top priority. Seth knew that Mel was a sick man. Until this moment, he hadn't realized the magnitude of his sickness. If he was capable of concocting a plan such as this, there was no telling of what else he was capable. (*Renée. Oh, my God. I have to get to Renée.*)

"Kathy," Seth said as calmly as possible, "where did Mel go after he *messed up* my car?" Kathy did not look up. "Kathy," Seth repeated, "you've already admitted to everything, so you better cooperate by telling me the truth. If you do, maybe I won't press charges against you for what you did to Princess."

He waited. Kathy finally looked up and said, "Even if you decide to try and press charges, I'm not worried because I'll find a way to get out of them. Just like Mel is planning on getting out of his. He has a plan you know." Seth did not say anything. He held his breath as he continued to wait patiently for her to continue. "Mel told me he had a few things to take care of after we took care of your car. You know, it doesn't really matter. Him and I are gonna have a happy life together. You can be angry with me all you want, but that's how it's gonna be. Really, Seth, you're going to have to accept this." She fiddled with the cheap costume jewelry ring that she was wearing on the ring finger of her left hand. Then dramatically she clutched her hands over her heart and relayed, "I never realized how much he meant to me until I almost lost him."

Seth, without acknowledging what Kathy had said, hurriedly left the office. "Official business, I'll be back as soon as I can!" he hollered to Hal, who was walking towards him eating a donut. Seth almost knocked him over as he ran out the door. All Seth could think about was Renée. He had to get to Renée before Mel got to her first. He dialed her number. He got her voice message. "Renée, Renée. It's Seth, pick up! Mel is out on bail, and he's coming after you. Renée, call me back as soon as you get this!" As he drove across town to the YMCA desperately trying to see through his cracked windshield, he called three different times. Still, she did not answer. Finally, he called information and got the number for the YMCA. All he got was an answering machine. "God, please keep her safe," he quietly prayed as he cut through traffic, trying to get across town as fast as possible. A million thoughts raced through his head. The words that Kathy had spoken echoed in his mind, 'I don't want this baby, and the baby's dad convinced me that you wouldn't want it either.' He couldn't believe she had lied to him about being the baby's father. (*What kind of sick person could do this? What kind of sick, demented woman would want a relationship with someone like Mel after everything he had done?*) Seth almost laughed, even though he found nothing comical in the situation.

Seth grabbed his phone again and called the YMCA one more time. To his relief, someone finally answered. "Hello, YMCA. This is Barb."

Seth tried desperately not to sound too frantic. "Hello, Barb. Could I speak to Renée, please?"

"Renée Kediner?"

"Yes."

"Um, who am I speaking to?" Barb asked.

"This is Seth. I'm a really good friend of hers, and I have to get a hold of her."

"Well," Beth answered hesitantly, "it's not really. . ."

"It's an emergency," Seth desperately interrupted. "Please?"

She paused for a moment and then answered, "Okay. She went home because she wasn't feeling very well,"

"How long ago?" Seth questioned.

"Oh, I don't know exactly, maybe about an hour ago."

"Okay, thank you. Thank you very much." As he hung up the phone, he quickly signaled, took the first right hand turn, spun his car around and headed for Renée's apartment. He just prayed it wasn't too late.

# Chapter XIV

Renée was tired and after her conversation with Seth, she was not feeling the greatest. Although she had just gotten to work, she had decided to go home. She would pick up Tyon from *Doggie Daycare* (a friend to whom she took him each morning, so he wouldn't have to be alone in the apartment), and the two of them would spend a relaxing day together. In the past seven years in which she had been employed as the Youth Director at the YMCA, she rarely missed a day. So when she explained to her supervisor that she was not feeling well and was going home, he had not raised too many objections.

Renée got into her car and turned off the radio. Not wanting to be disturbed by anyone, she shut off her cell phone. She was grateful for the quiet as she drove to her apartment. She couldn't remember the last time she got a good night's sleep, and as a result, she had been irritable, discontented, and just not her usual self. As she drove, she tried to clear her mind of everything and just concentrate on the solitude. Unfortunately, her mind could not erase the image of Mel's face, nor could she shut out the sound of his voice and the threats he had made. In the past, Renée had not been easily scared or threatened. But in the past, she had never been involved with anyone as conniving, manipulative, and vile as Mel. She wondered how long it would be before she would be able to let go of the fear and move on.

After she parked outside her apartment and locked her car, she and Tyon walked along the sidewalk to the back patio door. After Maggie and Seth had helped her move her belongings into the apartment, Maggie had been concerned about her living on the first floor. "Just make sure that you always keep the patio door locked and make sure you keep this pole or stick, or whatever it's called, in there. Okay?" Maggie had sternly advised Renée. "I'm worried about someone breaking in." Fiddling with the door she added, "It wouldn't be too difficult for someone to pry open this lock."

"I'll be fine," Renée had assured her. "You're such a worry wart."

Renée smiled at the memory as she found her key and unlocked the door. She and Tyon always went in the back way, so he could run for a while before going into their place. When she slid open the door, she was horrified at what she saw. Her apartment was in shambles. Her dining room table was overturned. All the cushions from the couch were thrown about the living room, and her television set and stereo were strewn about in pieces on the floor. "Oh, my God!" Renée screamed.

"Yeah, you pathetic whore, you better start praying," a voice came from the kitchen. There stood Mel, finishing a sandwich, and staring at Renée with a look of contempt and hate on his face.

Renée, thinking she would have a better chance of getting help if she ran out into the hallway, bolted towards the main door. Just as she got it open, Mel slammed it shut. But before he did, he kicked Tyon into the hallway and muttered, "I'll deal with one dog at a time." Then turning to Renée, he asked in an overly affectionate tone, "Planning on going somewhere, Renée?" He slowly walked towards her. "Were you gonna leave without even saying hello? Where's my hello kiss?" Renée kept slowly backing away from him, desperately looking from side to side, wondering if she could make it to the patio door before he caught her. She realized it was too late when he backed her into a corner in the kitchen. "Did you *really* think you were gonna get away with this? You're a nothing. A nobody. What're you gonna do now that your *boyfriend* isn't going to be here to save you? Well, I'll tell you what you're gonna do," he said as he finished the last bite of his sandwich. "You're gonna take what you got coming to you. That's what you're gonna do, you pathetic little slut."

"That's not my name," Renée said not recognizing her own voice.

"What?" Mel asked holding his hand to his ear. "What? Now you're questioning my intelligence? You don't think I know a piece of crap garbage ho like you when I see one? That's funny," he said as he cracked his knuckles, "real funny."

Renée felt like a caged animal as Mel kept slowly walking closer and closer to her. Her eyes frantically darted around the room, trying to think of something she could use as a weapon. Mel's eyes were red and his pupils were so wide that his blue irises were almost not visible. She did not know for certain, but he looked high, and she was terrified. She knew trying to reason with him would be useless, so she conserved her energy and waited apprehensively for him to make his next move.

"You know," he said glaring at her through the narrow slits where his eyes were, "I never really gave a crap about you. All you were to me was a two-bit whore." He laughed an evil laugh, and then continued, "Did you actually think someone like me could possibly love someone as worthless and pathetic as you? You are and always will be a useless nobody. And now I'm gonna give the dog what she's got coming to her." Mel lunged for Renée. She quickly moved out of the way and stuck out her foot. Mel tripped and rammed his head into the refrigerator. Renée wasted no time. She clasped her hands together over her head. Grunting, she brought them down square in the middle of Mel's back.

"You good for nothing bitch!" he wailed as he struggled to regain his balance. "Now you're really gonna get it!"

"Bring it on, loser!" Renée screamed. "I'm not scared of you!" She swiftly grabbed him by the shoulders, lifted her knee, and nailed him squarely in the groin.

He doubled over and fell to the floor.

She proceeded to kick him as hard as she could in the ribs. With each blow, Mel begged for mercy, but Renée was relentless as she turned him over and dug her knees into his chest. She angrily brought her arm back, and with everything in her, she punched him repeatedly in the face.

"Enough! Enough!" Mel cried trying to shield his face from Renée's blows.

"Shut up!" Renée sputtered through clenched teeth. "I'll let you know when it's enough!" Finally, when her hands bloody from the unrelenting blows, she got to her feet. Wiping the blood on her pants as she caught her breath she said in a powerful voice, "Get your pathetic loser ass off my floor and get out of my house. NOW!"

Mel moaned, rolled onto his hands and knees, and looked up at Renée. Blood was spilling from his mouth, "You're still nothing but a useless whore," he whispered.

"Oh, yeah?" Renée kicked him again in the ribs and exclaimed, "How do you like me now? Who's the worthless one now?"

But before Mel could answer, two policeman burst

through the door of the apartment with Tyon right behind them. "Freeze!" They pointed their guns at Mel. "Stay down there on the ground and put your arms and legs out to the side where we can see them!"

Mel stared at them in disbelief, but he begrudgingly did what he was told as one of the policemen slapped handcuffs on his wrists and dragged him out of the apartment.

"Are you okay, miss?" the other policeman questioned.

"I am now," she said letting out a sigh of relief as she picked up Tyon and hugged him close to her. "I am now."

Seth's car's tires squealed as he turned the corner and came to a stop in front of Renée's apartment building. He hurriedly raced from the abruptly stopped vehicle and sprinted to the main door. He barely stopped as he opened it and then ran to Renée's apartment door. It was slightly a jar. He pushed it opened, saw the chaotic state, and frantically called, "Renée! Renée! It's Seth! Are you here, Renée?"

Greeted at the door by Tyon, who welcomed him by wagging his tail, he saw Renée sitting calmly by the sink in the kitchen. At the recognition of his voice, she raised her head and gave him a smile. "Hi, Seth. Fancy meeting you here."

"What the . . . what the . . . ," he asked looking around. The disarray of her home made him furious. As he walked towards her, without meaning to, he angrily questioned, "What the hell happened?" Realizing the intensity with which he had asked his question, he softened his voice, knelt beside her, and asked more calmly, "Are you okay?"

Renée smiled while petting Tyon who had found a comfortable spot in her lap. "Better than I've been in a long time." He looked at her more closely. She no longer had the frightened look in her eyes. Instead, it was replaced with a calm, almost serene expression. "Seth," she said almost too casually.

"Yes?"

"Remember those self-defense moves you taught me so I could learn to protect myself?"

"Yeah," he said still kneeling in front of her.

"Well, they really work." She grabbed him around the neck and hugged him close to her.

"Okay, okay." Seth released Renée's grip around his neck and looked into her eyes that were filling with tears. He gently tucked her bangs behind her ear so they were out of her face and asked, "Do you want to tell me what happened?" He looked at her with concern wondering if she was in shock.

"I left work early, about an hour or so after I had gotten there. After talking to you on the phone, I just wasn't feeling too good. When I got home, my apartment was a disaster. But you can see that for yourself." She looked around, took a breath, and continued with her story. "I looked around, and Mel came out of the kitchen eating a sandwich."

"A sandwich?" Seth gave her a puzzled, confused look.

"Yeah, he ransacked my house, and then he had the nerve to steal my food. I was really upset," Renée stated looking seriously at Seth.

"Alright, then what happened?"

"I tried to run for the front door, because I thought there would've been a better chance of someone hearing me yelling for help. But just as I got it opened, Mel slammed it shut. But Tyon got out." She scratched Tyon's ear as he looked up and wagged his tail at her. "I thought about going for the patio door, but I thought if I made any sudden movement, that would be a good reason for Mel to attack me. That's when he backed me into a corner in the kitchen." Renée bit her lip to keep herself from crying.

Seth gently put a hand on her shoulder and encouraged her to continue. "What happened after that, Renée?"

"Seth, this is going to sound really odd, but I don't

really know. Well, I mean I know what I did, but I just don't know how."

Seth gave her a perplexed look. "You're going to have to be a little more specific."

"Okay," Renée sighed trying to put what happened into words. "Mel started telling me how worthless I was, and he started calling me all sorts of names. Then he said something like it's time for the dog to get its beating or time for the dog to get beat or something like that. That's when it happened."

"What happened, Renée?" Seth soothingly coaxed.

"Like I said, I don't really know how to explain it." Renée looked down and then up at Seth. "Seth, this is really weird, so please don't think I'm crazy, okay?"

"Okay," Seth willingly agreed.

"It was like I wasn't alone. It was like there was someone here with me who was going to protect me, and I was no longer afraid. I knew I was going to be okay." She took a deep breath and continued, "I figured Mel was high, and I didn't know what he was capable of doing. But I also knew that I had to stand up for myself otherwise I was going to live in fear for the rest of my life. Surprisingly, I remained really calm. When he came at me, I tripped him. He ran into the fridge, lost his balance, and I started attacking him. That sounds so harsh, Seth, but that's what I did. I knew that if I didn't hit him first, he was going to probably kill me." She looked into Seth's concerned eyes. "But I wasn't scared. Like I said, it was as if someone was here with me, protecting me. Anyway, after I literally beat the crap out of him, I told him to get out. I wasn't sure if he was going to come after me again, but I didn't have to find out because two cops showed up and took him away. The officers told me that the lady next door had heard Tyon barking. She came out of her apartment to see what was going on, because animals aren't supposed to be in the building. That's when she heard all the noise from the fight. Thank God she did, because she called 911." She stopped and looked at Seth. "You probably think I'm crazy."

"No, no. Not at all, Renée. Do you really want to know what I think?"

"Yes?"

"I think God helps those who help themselves."

"What?"

"Renée, you and Maggie asked me at one time what had changed in my life and how I came to be the man I am today. Do you remember what I told you?"

"Yes, you said it was God."

"Renée, on my way here, I repeatedly asked God to keep you safe. Now, whether you believe me or not is up to you, but I honestly know that He answered my prayer."

Renée sat in silence thinking about everything that had happened. Then she closed her eyes and contemplated what Seth had just explained to her. Finally, she asked, "Seth, do you really think that God was *here* with me? Do you think that that is what I felt, the feeling that I had like I wasn't alone?"

"Yes, Renée, "I really do."

Renée sat quietly. After a moment, she looked into his eyes and asked," A feeling like that happened to you too, Seth, didn't it? That's how you were able to change your life around."

"Yes."

"Do you ever talk about it?"

"Yes, with people who want to listen."

"I want to listen."

"Okay," Seth said getting up. He looked around the room. "I tell you what, let's get your place back in order, and then you and I can park ourselves on the couch, and I'll tell you all about it. The police will file a report, and they'll get the information to the insurance company. So let's start . . ." he looked around the room in disgust. (*What a mess that loser made.*) He exhaled loudly. "Let's start at that wall and work from there." He smiled and added, "Good thing you got rid or most of your stuff, otherwise we would be cleaning all night."

Renée smiled and nodded in agreement. She stood up and began, yet again, to put her life back together.

Renée and Seth sat by each other on the couch. Seth leaned back, patted the armrest and said, "Hey, this is the same couch you had in your old house. Glad to see you didn't get rid of it."

Renée smiled. She had gotten rid of a lot of things but not this couch. It was of sentimental value to her. It was on this very couch that she had finally admitted to herself how she truly felt about Seth. But she wasn't about to tell him that. "So are you going to tell me what happened?"

"I was pretty bad into drugs, to the point that I started selling them to support my habit," Seth glanced at Renée and continued. "It was going great, at first. I had lot of money, and I had a lot of power. I was in charge of a ring of sellers, but there was always something missing. I thought that the more drugs I did and the more money I made would take that feeling away, but it didn't." He sadly looked down and quietly stated, "Nothing ever did. I was never truly happy. No matter how many material possessions I had, it was never enough."

"Wow," Renée said as Seth paused. "Seth, I never would've thought. So how did you change? How did you get to be who you are today?"

"I'm getting to that," Seth smiled. He knew patience was not one of Renée's strong characteristics. "A drug deal went bad, really bad. A kid got shot, and I was the one to find him. Seeing his body lying on the floor of the alley dropped me to my knees. His eyes were open, staring up at the dark sky, and a pool of blood was around him. An overwhelming feeling of emptiness and fear overtook me.

For the first time in- well, I couldn't even guess when- I folded my hands and prayed. I can't tell you exactly what I said, but I can tell you what happened. I felt as if arms were wrapped around me, holding me. Although my life was more chaotic than it ever had been, I got the feeling that everything was going to be okay. I cried, Renée, something I had not been able to do for years. I cried like a baby. I knew something had to change. I got up and started aimlessly wandering around in the night. I had no idea where I was planning on going." He paused for a while, recalling the life changing memory, and then honestly said, "I'd never been much of a believer in God or anything religious, but it was as if a power beyond my control led me to a church. It was late. When I got there, a man dressed in a robe- I had assumed he was a priest or a monk or something- met me at the door. As odd as it sounds, it was as if he had been waiting for me. I don't know what came over me, but I felt so comfortable and safe in his presence that I told him all that had happened. I talked with that gentle, forgiving man until light started showing through the stained glass windows. And," he smiled as he continued, "I was particularly impressed with a certain stained glass window." He thought about the conversation he and Renée had had after attending a Sunday Mass. It was when she had told him about the church she had gone to with her grandma when she was younger. "Want to guess what was on it?"

A smile spread across Renée's face as she recalled the time she had told Seth about attending Mass with her grandmother when she was a young girl. She looked at him and knew they were each recalling the same memory. "I bet it was the picture of Jesus knocking at the door," Renée answered with certainty.

Seth confirmed her answer by smiling and nodding his head. Then he went on to tell the rest of his story. "Physically, emotionally, and although I didn't know it at the time, spiritually exhausted, I fell asleep in the pew we were sitting in. I was woken up when someone poked me in my shoulder. I looked around for the man I had been talking to, but he was nowhere. When I asked the man, who had poked me- he turned out to be the janitor- where the other guy was, he scratched his head and gave me a puzzled look. He said no one had been in the church since about seven o'clock the night before." Seth gave Renée some time to absorb what he had said before he went on. "Now, I'm not sure what time I came to that church, but I know it was long after seven." He paused again, folded his hands in front of him, and then intently stared into Renée's eyes. "Renée, I'm not saying that I'm in a position to say who that man was, but I can tell you this, that experience changed my life. Afterwards, I knew I had no choice but to get my act together. So I checked myself into rehab, and afterwards I went back to college. Luckily, I had my generals done before I started leading that kind of life, so I didn't have to start completely over. I finished my degree, and with a lot of luck, I landed a decent job. But no matter where I go or what I do, that memory never leaves me. It's something I'll never forget."

Renée looked understandingly at Seth. Now it was all starting to make sense. Helping out at the soup kitchen, coaching soccer, volunteering his time and energy; it was all an attempt to give back, a way to say thank you for what had been given to him- a second chance. He had a new lease on life, and with it, he had the ability to intuitively handle all types of absurd problems and situations at which others might be baffled. She rested her head on his shoulder. She wanted to tell him of the love she had for him, how at first she thought it was a mere crush, a foolish attraction, but over time she knew it was so much more. She had fought the feelings, not believing that anything good would come out of her acting on them. There was so much about him which she loved: his smile, his eyes, his sense of humor, his honesty and integrity. But most of all, she loved that fact that he was her best friend. She turned to him with love in her eyes and a deep felt intensity in her heart, but he had fallen asleep. Instead of trying to wake him, she curled up under his arm, thanking God for all the gifts which He had given her.

"Renée, Renée," Seth nudged her gently, "what time is it?"

"Uh, I don't know," Renée said between yawns. "What're you still doing here?"

"I guess I fell asleep," Seth said gently touching her face. "But I really need to get home and get to bed. My job might not be the greatest in the world, but it's a job. And I already was warned about missing too many days." He grabbed the blanket off the back of the couch and laid it over Renée who was comfortably curled up and drifting back to sleep.

"Are you going to be okay? Do you want me to stay here with you?"

"No, no," Renée answered sleepily. "I'll be okay." Between yawns she asked, "Will you set my alarm and lock the door when you leave?" Not waiting for Seth's response, she fell back asleep.

"Of course," Seth said getting up. He kissed Renée lightly on the forehead, "Good night, princess, sweet dreams."

"Mmmmm," Renée drowsily said. Then, to Seth's astonishment, she added, "Good night, I love you."

Seth stood for a moment, completely bewildered. (*Did she just say what I think she said?*) Suddenly, he was completely alert and awake. He seemingly floated to her room to set her alarm. Coming back into the living room, he glanced at her one more time. He took his key ring from his pocket, and made sure he still had the key Renée had given to him when she had moved in. An enormous smile spread across his face as he quietly locked the door and shut it behind him. Leaning against the closed door, he felt as if his heart was going to beat out of his chest. "She loves me," he said in a whisper. "Renée loves me."

# Chapter XV

Mel was brought directly down to the station; the one from which he had been released before being taken to the local jail. He lay on the plastic mat in the holding cell. He stared at the ceiling and shook his head from side to side. He hated her. He hated Renée so badly that he wished, when he had had the chance, that he had killed her. He smiled at the thought of her lifeless body lying dead and him triumphantly standing over her. He laughed and said aloud, "It would've saved me a lot of headaches, that's for sure."

"What're you mumbling about?" the guard asked as he glanced in Mel's direction.

"Shut the hell up," Mel said as he rolled on his side and faced the wall. "I wouldn't even be in here if it wasn't for that dumb whore."

"She had nothing to do with the choices you made." Mel cocked his head back. Standing outside his cell was his dad.

"Pop!" Mel excitedly said as he got to his feet. Holding

onto the bars and trying to poke his head through, he imploringly looked up at his dad. "You're going to get me out of here, right, Pop?"

Adam shook his head from side to side, looked Mel in the eyes, and said, "Not this time, son. Not this time."

In a fit of rage, Mel slammed into the bars. "What? What do you mean? You're gonna leave your own child locked in a cage? What kind of parent are you?" He looked directly into his dad's eyes as he had a thousand times before searching for any weakness that would allow him to pounce. His dad appeared unwavering. So pretending that he was close to tears, Mel deliberately softened his tone and begged, "Come on, Pop. I need you to pull some strings and get me out of here!"

Adam took a deep breath; he was at a loss for words. With tears in his eyes, he looked at Mel. "Mel, I've tried everything I could to be a good father to you. I've always given in to you, even when you were young. In the past you've always gotten your way, but not this time."

"What?" Mel asked in disbelief. "What?" he repeated questioning if he had correctly heard his dad's response.

"Not this time, Mel. This time, you've really done it." Adam closed his eyes and rubbed the back of his neck. After a moment, he opened them and looked at Mel. "I've hired an attorney for you. He's one of the best around the area. I've briefly talked with him about your circumstances. He said if you accept a plea bargain, the best case scenario is that you'll serve three to five years in prison."

"What? That's all you're gonna do? Pop," Mel pleaded, "you *have* to get me out of here!"

"And then what?" Adam said slightly raising his voice in frustration and anger. "Then what, Mel? Then you go after Renée again? What were your intentions last time going to her home? What were you planning on doing? This has got to stop, Mel. I've done everything I've known how to help you, to give you a better life. But you repeatedly make bad choices. What do you suggest I do, Mel?" He briefly stared at him, not really expecting an answer, and then he turned to leave.

"Pop! Don't leave me! Don't go! I didn't mean for this to happen, really. I love Renée, and I want her back. I was going to her apartment so we could work things out."

Adam stopped and folded his arms across his chest. Without turning around he stated, "That's a lie, Mel, and you know it."

Feeling the tears forming in his eyes, he walked out of the station. His head hung low as he recalled the conversation he had had with his son. (*Am I doing the right thing? Was it wrong for me to leave and walk away?*) He stopped and felt in his suit jacket for his wallet. He took out the card that the lawyer had given him. He turned it over and over in his hand before putting it away. "Maybe he'll be able to help you," he commented quietly and then carefully tucked his wallet back into his pocket.

When he looked up, a short, blonde woman coming up the stairs ran directly into him. He caught her before she lost her balance, but, unbeknownst to Adam, not before she slid her hand inside his jacket and snatched his wallet that she had seen him holding. "Oh, excuse me, miss," Adam apologized as he steadied her. "Are you okay?"

"No worries," she said, smirking at him as she hurried up the stairs.

Adam unlocked his car, got inside, and set his head on the steering wheel. (*What am I going to do now?*) He reached for his wallet to take out the card so he could call Mel's lawyer. He knew he had just placed it in the inside pocket of his suit jacket, but it was gone. He looked anxiously around the car but still could not find it. He took a deep breath in attempt to calm himself. He had just had it. Then, knowingness came over him. He hurriedly got out of the car and ran up the stairs from which he had just come.

"Sir?" the bailiff asked as Adam walked in the door.

"Can I help you, again?"

"Yes," Adam said, "I'm here to see my son."

The bailiff gave him a confused look, shook his head, and responded, "Follow me."

Turning the corner, Adam saw the blonde lady for the second time that day. Just as he suspected, she was in deep conversation with his son.

"Pop," Mel said with false sincerity, "coming back to visit me so soon?"

"Not really," Adam said turning his attention from Mel to the blonde. "Give me my wallet."

"What?" she asked trying to look innocent.

"Now!"

"Oh," she said digging in her purse, "this is *yours*? I just found it outside the station on the stairs when I was coming in to visit Mel."

"Sure you did," Adam mumbled as he snatched the wallet from her outstretched hand.

"Wow, Pop," Mel said winking at the blonde lady, "the least you could do is thank Kathy for picking it up for you."

Disgusted, Adam looked from Mel to Kathy and back to Mel again. "What've you gotten yourself into now?"

"Pop, this is my friend, Kathy."

Smiling, Kathy turned to Adam and held out her hand. "Nice to meet you again."

Adam did not shake her hand. Instead he turned his attention to Mel and with disgust in his voice questioned, "Don't you think you're in enough trouble the way it is?"

"What're you talking about, Pop? She's just a friend."

Furious, Adam had to leave the room. Ignoring Mel's protests as he turned around to walk out, he thought of all Mel had put Renée through. And now this was just adding insult to injury. He wondered how long Mel had been sneaking around seeing this woman. Had she been part of the reason why Mel had so angrily attacked Renée? Adam shook his head; he just couldn't understand Mel. (*Why is he never satisfied with what he has? Why is it that he always assumes the grass is always so much greener somewhere else?*)

Kathy folded her arms in front of her chest, tapped her foot, stuck out her lip and stated, "Mel, your dad doesn't like me."

"Sure he does, baby," Mel said looking at her up and down. "Who wouldn't? He was just a little pissed that you took his wallet."

Kathy moved her arms to her hips, opened her mouth in disbelief, and snottily said, "Uh, Mel, I didn't take it. I *found* it on the steps outside. I was gonna turn it into the guard when I left."

"Okay, okay, I believe you. You don't have to get your panties all in a bundle over it. You know?" Mel leaned against the bars of the cell. "Well, did you use the money I got for you to take care of that little problem?"

"Uh, well, not exactly," she stammered. "I think we need to talk more about that. Yeah, I think I really wanna have this baby." She shrugged her shoulders and looked with question at Mel. "Do you think you might change your mind, Mel?"

"Kathy," Mel remarked trying not to lose his patience, "we talked about this. I thought you understood that in order for us to start a life together, we need to start out just the two of us. A baby would just . . . it would just . . . it would cramp our style. We wouldn't be able to go out and do all the cool stuff I've planned. It'd be a lot easier to get rid of it now since you're not too far along." He began insidiously laughing as he stated, "God, Seth was stupid for believing this. What a dumb ass. Don't you think?"

Kathy giggled in agreement. "No kidding! We really had him going, didn't we?" She laughed for a moment longer, and then began to consider what Mel had been saying. Knowing she was not going to change his mind, she finally gave in. "Okay, Mel, I'll do it. But I don't wanna go by myself."

"Okay, okay. How about as soon as I get out of here, the second place we go is to get that taken care of?"

"You promise?" Kathy asked pushing her lips outward. "And where will be the first place we go?"

Mel smiled, and emitted an evil laugh. "I guess you'll just have to wait and see, but I guarantee it'll be worth the wait. Oh, how it'll be worth it." His eyes were set in an eerie gaze as he cracked his knuckles."

"Oh, a surprise!" Kathy clapped her hands. "I really like the sound of that. I love surprises!" Then she lowered her eyes and began to pout. "How long do you think you'll be in here? I've been getting lonely, and I can't keep holding off the urge to be with other guys forever."

"I know, I know," Mel patronizingly sympathized with her. "And believe me, you won't have to."

"Alright, time's up," the guard gestured to Kathy. "Time for you to leave. The only reason you were allowed in is because of your relation to the inmate."

"Just one more minute, please?" Kathy asked batting her eyelashes.

"Say your goodbyes and then leave." The guard said without hesitation. He remained stationary, waiting to escort Kathy out if necessary.

Not getting her way, Kathy glared at him. Realizing her time was limited, she turned her attention to Mel. "Can't wait to see you again," she whispered, leaning closer to him. "Oh, how I love you."

Mel gave her an irritated look and replied, "Yeah, Kathy, yeah, whatever."

She flipped her blonde hair over her shoulder as she haughtily turned and walked past the guard.

# Chapter XVI

The bail hearing had been set. But unfortunately for Mel, due to the fact that he had tampered with state's witnesses, his bail had been denied. The trial date had been scheduled for the following week. During the time before the trial, Mel was being held without bond.

The day after the bail hearing, the high priced lawyer his dad had hired for him showed up at the jail to go over his defense. Mel waited angrily in the small room. He was still bruiting about the unjust way he felt his dad had treated him.

The door opened and in walked Mel's lawyer, Ben Hillman, the best defense lawyer in the state. He was by whom every criminal wanted to be represented. Ben's demeanor was subtle, but powerful. His cold, steel eyes cut through Mel like a torch as he stared at him over wire rimmed glasses. He was a tall man, dressed impeccably in a tailor made suit. Mel felt inferior and uneasy in his presence.

Ben carefully set down his briefcase, stared at Mel, and

then said, "I think we should deal."

(*This is the great attorney's advice, to take a plea bargain?* Mel wanted to say, but thought better of it.) He slouched in his chair and remarked with emphasis, "I *can't* go back to prison."

Ben opened his briefcase and took out a file. Opening it and flipping through the material, he looked up at Mel and stated matter-of-fact, "I've gone over the evidence and the facts. We can try some razzle-dazzle, but it's a pretty open and shut case."

Mel rocked back in his chair, and then angrily looked at Ben. "I don't care. There's gotta be a way to get me out of this. Money's not an issue. My dad's willing to pay for whatever it takes."

"Maybe you're not understanding me," Ben abruptly cut into Mel's remark. "It's not about money. It's about the facts. The best we could do would be to make the facts look fuzzy for the perspective jurors, and even without your criminal record, that would be a long shot."

Mel replied cockily, "All we need is one for a mistrial, and I'm willing to take my chances."

"Okay," Ben said shuffling his papers and putting them back in his briefcase. Standing up he continued, "Looks like you've made your decision." As he reached for the door handle he stopped, looked over his shoulder at Mel, and added, "Just for the record, they *are* offering four years." (Closing the door as he exited the room, Ben thought, *that'd be a hell of a deal for you, you arrogant, self-centered, spoiled brat. Unfortunately, you're too stupid to figure that out.*)

A few days later, Ben returned to the jail to go over Mel's defense. As they sat in the same small room, Ben tried again to make Mel realize it would be in his best interest to accept the plea bargain. To Ben's irritation and annoyance, Mel arrogantly answered, "You work for me. My dad's paying you good money. You've a reputation of being the best defense lawyer in the state, so what's your deal? Scared? That doesn't seem like part of your résumé. I wanna get out of this damned cage and not come back. Now, how're you gonna do that?"

Ben could feel his temperature rise as he struggled to keep his composure. Instead of reaching across the table, grabbing the little punk and knocking him on his arrogant ass like he wanted to do, he took a deep breath. Finally, after staring at Mel until he uncomfortably squirmed in his seat, Ben responded, "Listen and listen well. You may believe you're above the law just because your dad's rich, but I've news for you. I can drop this stinking case any time I want. Believe it or not, I've even more money than your dad. I took on this case as a personal favor for him, not because I particularly like you. In fact, I can hardly stand to be in the same room as you. Now the way I look at it, you have two choices. One, you knock it off with the pompous attitude, and we try and build a defense or two, I leave and you can try to find another lawyer who'd be willing to represent you in such a cut and dried case."

Mel's first reaction was to tell Ben to screw off. But instead, he managed to keep his mouth shut, nodded his head, and said between clenched teeth, "Okay, I'll cooperate."

The night before the trial was to begin, Maggie, and Renée found themselves sitting at their table at the coffee shop. Renée had been anxious all day and was relieved when the three of them had decided to sit down all together, visit, and try to relax. All of them had been subpoenaed to take the stand at some point during the trial. Maggie and Seth took it in stride, but the thought of having to relive the events that had transpired made Renée apprehensive and nervous. She knew it was the only way justice could be served, but yet, she was still uneasy about being in the courtroom with the man who had not only threatened to kill her once, but twice.

"How was work?" Seth asked earnestly as he looked from Maggie to Renée.

"Good, good," Maggie replied noisily sipping her cappuccino. "My clientele is really picking up, so it's kind of a double edged sword. You know? I mean it's wonderful from the financial aspect, but at the end of some of the long days, my feet are killing me."

Renée smiled. (*What would she do without Maggie?*) "Uh, it was okay. At least it keeps my mind off of things," she somberly admitted.

"How long do you think the trial will last?" Maggie asked. "How much time do you think we'll need off of work? I need to start arranging my schedule."

"Not sure, depends a lot on the testimony of the people on the stand. Honestly, I don't think too long. Apparently Mel didn't want to take a plea bargain or anything, which is rather stupid considering all the evidence against him, but what'd you expect?" Seth asked.

The first day of trial, Maggie, Seth, and Renée all met at the courthouse and walked in together. Seth calmly took Renée's hand in his and the two of them followed Maggie to where she found a place to sit. Renée was relieved to realize that the courtroom was not overcrowded with people as she was accustomed to seeing on TV. The three of them sat behind the prosecuting attorney's table and waited patiently for the judge to enter the courtroom. Hearing the doors open behind them, Renée turned to see Mel being escorted by two guards to his seat next to his attorney in the front of the courtroom. He was dressed in an orange jumpsuit. The beginning of a beard shadowed his face. He sneered at Renée as he walked by and mouthed, "Dumb bitch."

Seth could feel Renée's body tense, and he whispered softly, "It's going to be okay." Renée looked up into his eyes and nodded her head in agreement.

Throughout the next three days, Maggie, Renée, and Seth all took the stand. They honestly relayed what had happened. Finally, on the fourth day, the closing arguments were heard, and the court was to reconvene as soon as the jury conclusively reached a verdict on the numerous charges against Mel.

After deliberating for just one hour, the jury returned.

Ben sat in silence. (He closed his eyes, shook his head, and thought, *this is not good*.) Because of the short amount of time the jury had been mulling over the facts of the case, Ben knew the verdict would not be innocent nor would there be the remote chance that there would be a hung jury. He knew beyond a doubt that the verdict would be read as guilty- unfortunately for Mel- it would probably be on all counts. Ben lifted his head and looked sympathetically to his client. Quickly his sympathy turned to disbelief when he observed Mel winking and waving to a blonde sitting two rows back from the defense table.

"Knock it off," Ben said in a stern, irritated whisper. "They're about to read the verdict."

Mel let out an annoyed grunt. "Yeah whatever, buddy," he said as he again turned and smiled at the blonde. Then he said to Ben, "I don't need you anymore, so why don't you just lay off? I'll be found innocent. Any fool knows that especially considering how little time the jury was out."

Yet again, Ben was placed in a position where it took every ounce of self-control not to grab this brat by the scruff of the neck and try to beat some sense into him

As the bailiff took the ruling from the judge and handed it back to the jury foreman, everyone's eyes in the courtroom were on Mel. Mel sat confidently in his chair with his arm draped over the back of it

The judge asked, "Count one, first degree possession, how do find the defendant?"

"Guilty," the jury foreman said somberly.

Mel, expecting it to be not guilty, started to stand up to celebrate. Then the realization hit him that the jury foreman had said *guilty*. His mind raced. (*How could this have happened?* He felt a cold sweat trickle down his back. He screamed inside his head, *I can't go back to prison! I narked on some people, and they're gonna be in there waiting for me!*) He sat dumbstruck with a look of silent desperation, and then he realized that there were more verdicts that were still yet to be read.

"Count two, felon in possession of a firearm, how do you find the defendant?" Kathy dug her fingernails under her seat. She looked from Mel to the jury foreman and back again to Mel. (*Although he's guilty on the first count, maybe he'll get probation, community service, limited time in jail, or anything. I'm still pregnant . . . what'll I do if he gets sent away to prison?*)

"Guilty," the jury foreman echoed the first verdict.

"Count three, possession of a stolen fire arm?"

Maggie looked over at Mel then to Renée and back to Mel. For a brief moment, she felt sorry for him. (*What kind of a man could ever stoop so low to hurt someone as beautiful and wonderful as Renée?*) Then she remembered Renée, huddled in her arms, terrified for her life. (*The son-of-a-bitch is getting exactly what he deserves*, Maggie thought as she crossed her arms across her chest.)

"Guilty," was the same reply.

"Count four, felony tampering with state's witness?"

Seth, sitting next to Renée for the entire sentencing, felt her tense up beside him. He looked at her, cupped his hand over hers and whispered, "It's going to be okay." (*This must be hell on her,* he thought as he looked at Mel*, but at least now she'll be free of the asshole.*)

"Guilty," the word was restated.

"Count five, felony tampering with a state's witness?"

Adam sat quietly, his hands folded in front of him. (*I know he's guilty of all the charges. But, God, please have them be merciful.*) After the jury had returned so quickly, he had looked at Ben, Mel's lawyer. When he had seen the expression on his face, Adam knew things were a lot worse than even Ben had anticipated. In the past, Adam had always been able to step in and relieve Mel from the majority of the consequences that his actions had encored. However, he knew this time that would not be the case. There was not enough money in his bank account, or the world for that matter, to reverse the resounding responses spoken in that courtroom.

"Guilty."

"Count six, gross misdemeanor, domestic assault?"

Renée finally opened her eyes, and for the first time since the sentencing started, looked directly at Mel. She did not feel angry, afraid, or even happy about the verdicts thus far. What she felt was numb. Sitting before her was a man whom she truly believed she had loved. One with whom she had been willing to commit her entire life. She desperately tried to dismiss from her mind any adoring memories because the truth of the matter was that he had threatened to kill her. She continued to stare at Mel. (*I wonder what he's feeling- remorse? regret? fear? No*, she finally decided, *what he's feeling is sorry for himself. Like endless times before, he's taking no personal responsibility for any of his actions. The court has proven him guilty beyond a reasonable doubt, and sadly, all he'll continue to do is blame everyone else for what he's done.*)

"Guilty."

The judge cleared his throat and relayed the facts speaking directly to Mel, "The maximum time on all counts is fifteen years in federal prison. If there was any way I could give you more, I would. But since I can't, I'm sentencing you to the maximum. Sentence starts immediately." The judge slammed down his gavel and said, "Court adjourned."

As Mel was being led away, he repeatedly tried to

struggle free as he screamed, "This ain't fair! It ain't right! This is a bunch of bull! What's wrong with you people?"

After Mel was gone, Kathy began walking towards Seth whimpering, "Oh, Seth, Seth, I never really loved him. It was always you I wanted."

Seth did not even dignify her with a response. He brushed past her with Maggie and Renée on either side and hurriedly walked out of the courtroom."

"You mean you're just going to leave me? What am I supposed to do?"

Seth stopped, turned around, and remarked with a tone Renée had never heard him use, "What? You're asking me what you're supposed to do. Unbelievable, Kathy. Unbelievable. You turn everyone's lives completely upside down- especially mine- and then you have the nerve to ask me what you're going to do?

"But, Seth," Kathy whined, tears streaming down her face, "you loved me once. You did. I know it. Can you honestly say that I mean nothing to you?"

He turned and walked away. Maggie and Renée, extremely uncomfortable in this predicament, turned to follow Seth who looked like he was in a hurry to leave before he punched someone.

"Renée!" Kathy called. "Renée!"

Maggie grabbed her arm and pleaded with her eyes. "Don't. Don't even go there, just keep on walking."

"He's never going to care about you the way he did me. He'll never love you. He'll just use you and leave you!" Kathy screamed after them, but they didn't even turn to acknowledge her. Instead they went outside to find Seth.

He was leaning up against his car smoking a cigarette.

"I thought you quit," Maggie commented.

"I did," Seth said inhaling. "Now, isn't it about time we get out of here?"

"Yeah," Renée and Maggie agreed. The three of them got into Seth's Camaro.

"Sure you're okay to drive?" Maggie asked Seth with concern.

"Yeah, Maggie, yeah, I'm okay. He held open the door. As Maggie climbed in the backseat, he said to Renée, "Sure *you* don't want to drive?"

Appreciating the lightness in his tone, Renée slightly laughed and said, "Maybe another day, Seth. Maybe another day."

"Where to?" Seth asked glancing in the review mirror at Maggie and then looking over to Renée.

"Joe's Place sound good? Have you guys been there since it opened?" Maggie asked from the back seat.

Seth and Renée looked at each other and both shook their heads that they hadn't.

"Okay, Joe's Place it is. I tell you, I'm definitely up for something good to eat and to kick back and relax. That was pretty intense today, wasn't it?" Maggie went on to comment.

Renée, playing with the handle of her purse sadly stated, "Goodbyes usually are." She leaned her head against the window. Shutting her eyes, she let the tears slowly slide down her cheeks. She earnestly hoped this would be the end to the tears she would cry over Mel.

When she finally opened them, she was surprised to see that they had already arrived at Joe's Place. The ride that should have taken ten to fifteen minutes seemed to have been over in the blink of an eye.

Renée sat up and opened the mirror on the visor. As she stared at her reflection, she noticed her eyes were slightly puffy from crying. She impatiently cleaned the dried mascara from her cheeks, and searched through her purse for her tube of lipstick. "I look like crap," she said with a light laugh then turned towards Seth who was staring at her.

"That's not true," he whispered softly. "I've never seen you look more beautiful." If Maggie wouldn't have been so impatient to get out of the car, he would have wrapped her in his arms and kissed her right there. Renée blushed as her brown eyes sparkled.

"Okay, okay, we're here!" Maggie called impatiently while pushing on the back of Seth's seat. "Let me out, I'm hungry."

Laughing, Seth got out and held the car door open for Maggie. "Sorry, Maggie, I wouldn't want to stand in the way of you and your food. They way you eat, I swear you should weigh at least three hundred pounds."

Maggie, who was already out of the car, turned around and stuck her tongue out at Seth. Laughing at her immaturity, Renée and Seth watched her walk in the front door of Joe's place.

"Gotta love her, skinny as she is and all," Renée laughed as she put her lipstick back into her purse. She sat silently for a while, then looked at Seth and said, "Okay, I'm ready."

As soon as Seth and Renée entered Joe's Place, Renée immediately began to feel at ease. The atmosphere made her feel at home and comfortable. It was a nice, welcoming change from the intensity of the courtroom. Renée waited for her eyes to adjust to the dimmer light as she looked around the large dining area. Round tables set on a hardwood floor were covered with red and white checked table cloths. Behind the swinging door was the kitchen where Renée could hear the distinct sound of the grill hissing as it cooked Joe's homemade burgers. In one corner was an old fashioned juke box, and along the side wall was a bar complete with swivel barstools.

Renée felt like she had gone back in time as she and Seth weaved through the tables of people to Maggie who was sitting at the bar inhaling a burger.

"Preferential treatment?" Seth asked from behind Maggie.

"You bet," she said between bites. "I've a good man who treats me right."

"I guess you weren't kidding when you said you were hungry." Renée laughed as she sat on a barstool beside Maggie.

"I called Joe ahead of time on my cell phone. I would've ordered for the two of you, but I wasn't sure what you wanted. Joe is in the kitchen, but I can get one of the waitresses to get your order."

"Sounds good," Seth said eyeing an elevated corner table. "Hey, you guys mind if we sit over there?" He gestured to the table.

"No problem," Maggie said grabbing her plate and moving. "So what do you guys think?"

"Nice, really nice," Renée said and Seth nodded in agreement. "It really has a nice "homey" feel. I like it a lot. For the first time today, I feel like I can let my guard down and relax."

"I'm not going to offer an opinion until I get to taste the food." Seth winked at Renée while grabbing one of Maggie's fries.

"Hey!" She laughed as she swatted at his hand and missed. "Get your own!"

"I would if a waitress would show up!"

"How about a waiter?" said a voice came from behind them. They all looked up into the smiling face of Joe.

"Hey, Joe," Seth said turning around to shake his hand. "Nice, really nice place you have here."

"Hmmmm," Joe said after giving Maggie a kiss on the cheek, "thought you weren't going to make a judgment until you tasted the food."

"Ah," Seth embarrassedly said.

Joe started laughing. "Don't worry about it, Seth. I ordered you guys a few appetizers. They should be out in a minute. Just something to tie you over until you decide what you want. Sorry Maggie is being so rude. She selfishly eats her food in front of you, and she's not even sharing."

"Hey!" Maggie exclaimed as she punched Joe in the arm. "Be nice!"

As the appetizers arrived, Joe apologized that he had to get back to work. "Things should slow down in a bit, and I'll come back and sit with you guys when it does, okay?" He then put his arm gently over Renée's shoulders and told her softly, "Renée, I'm sure this hasn't been easy for you, but I'm so grateful that you're okay." He kissed her on the forehead before leaving to go back to work. Renée watched him as he walked away towards the kitchen. (*He is such a kind, sincere person. Maggie is truly blessed with having him in her life.*) He stopped at tables along the way, conversing briefly with his customers. He smiled with gratitude as they told him how good the food was and about the relaxed atmosphere.

After ordering, it didn't take long for their food to arrive. Renée's eyes got big as she stared at all the food on her plate. As she took a bite from her burger, she remembered that the last thing she had eaten was biscotti at the coffee house the night before which now seemed like years ago instead of just a twenty-four hour period. Maggie and Seth were engaged in conversation, but she silently ate as she thought of everything that had happened in the last twelve hours or so. Although it saddened her, thoughts of Mel kept entering her mind. He was going to be locked up for a long time. In spite of the fact that Renée was grateful that she would be safe, she still felt somewhat sorry for him. (*Maybe given some time to think and contemplate what he had done will help straighten him out.* She sighed. *No, unfortunately, not even that'll help him to change.*)

Then she glanced across the table at Seth. She stopped and looked at him; really looked at him. In the time she had known him, she could hardly believe all they had been through. And they had stood by each other during all of it. (*It's apparent he feels the same way about me as I do him. But how do we go forward? How do we take the next step?*)

As she was considering her questions, *Angel Eyes* by the Jeff Healey Band started playing from the jukebox in the corner of the restaurant. "Oh, I love this song," Renée quietly stated.

When Renée spoke, Seth looked up. Even though her eyes were still slightly puffy from crying, she looked absolutely beautiful. (*Kind of like a classic car- what you see is what you get.*). "Is that a suggestion to ask you to dance?" Seth inquired, smiling at her as he raised an eyebrow

Wondering when he had mastered that trick, Renée looked at him from across the table and finally said, "Only if you want to."

He stood up and held out his hand. Renée grasped it as he led her out to the dance floor.

"About damned time," Renée could hear Maggie annoyingly comment to Joe who had joined her at the table. "Do you think they're *finally* going to get together?"

Renée did not even bother to respond. Seth took her lightly in his arms, and she gently rested her head on his chest. For the first time in her life, a feeling came over her that she could not completely put into words. She briefly looked down at her feet to make sure that they were still touching the ground because she felt like she was floating. Her head felt light and airy almost like it was lightly wrapped in silk. (*This must be what love truly feels like.*) She tilted her head and looked up into Seth's loving and understanding dark eyes. "So, where do we go from here?"

Seth pulled her closely to him, gently kissed her, and then whispered, "Where ever God decides to take us."

The End

Printed in the United States
204076BV00001B/151-165/P